Here's what  critics

Catheri ne Brud's boo

"I highly recommend this series, and this book is one of the best!"
—*Kings River Life Magazine*

"Readers are sure to enjoy this playful tale...this book is bound to please anyone that is looking for an easy, satisfying read on the beach."
—*InD'tale Magazine*

"If you like your cozy mysteries complete with a cast of zany characters this is one for you. And guess what? Recipes are included which makes me really wish I could bake."
—*Night Owl Reviews*

"TASTES LIKE MURDER is an intriguing start to the *Cookies and Chance Mystery* series. I want to visit more with all of the quirky characters just to see what crazy and outrageous things they will do next!"
—*Fresh Fiction*

"Twistier than expected cozy read—great for beach or by the fire"
—*The Kindle Book Review*

BOOKS BY CATHERINE BRUNS

Cookies & Chance Mysteries:
Tastes Like Murder
"A Spot of Murder"
(short story in the Killer Beach Reads collection)
Baked to Death
Burned to a Crisp
Frosted with Revenge
Silenced by Sugar
"Drizzle Before Dying"
(short story in the Pushing Up Daisies collection)
Crumbled to Pieces
Sprinkled in Malice
Ginger Snapped to Death
Icing on the Casket

Cindy York Mysteries:
Killer Transaction
Priced to Kill
For Sale by Killer

Aloha Lagoon Mysteries:
Death of the Big Kahuna
Death of the Kona Man

Icing on the Casket

A Cookies & Chance Mystery

USA TODAY BESTSELLING AUTHOR
CATHERINE BRUNS

To Kathy, for the inspiration, and thinking outside the box.

Acknowledgements

A very special thank you to Kim Davis for creating the coffin cookie (apple spice) recipe and for allowing her photographs to be incorporated into the cover art! I am in awe of your talent.

My deepest gratitude to retired Troy police Captain Terrance Buchanan for answering my never-ending questions. Thank you to the dynamic duo of Constance Atwater and Kathy Kennedy for beta reading and to Amy Reger for the use of her delicious recipes. Last but not least a very special thanks to my husband Frank, who puts up with me and my pretend little world, where I often take him along for the ride.

CHAPTER ONE

———

My eyes flickered open with a start, an immediate sense of dread washing over me. I stared into the darkness, waiting for the inevitable to happen.

The room was quiet, except for Mike's soft snoring in my ear. Spike, our 15-year-old Shih Tzu, was stretched across the bottom of the bed in a soft furry lump that connected with my foot when I moved it. Bleary eyed, I turned to stare at the alarm clock on my nightstand. The big, red numbers flashed three thirty.

Any second now it would happen. I tried to brace myself. Like the captain of the Titanic approaching the iceberg, I'd accepted my certain fate. I waited with bated breath and counted to ten in my head. One…two…three. My heart pounded rapidly against the wall of my chest. Four…five…six…

A whimper filled the room, followed by a sharp cry. *Waah, waah.*

I stared at the baby monitor next to the clock, its light flashing. Yep, she was right on schedule. My baby daughter never disappointed.

I glanced to my left, waiting to see if there was any sign of life from my husband. His chest rose and fell in time with his snoring. It was wrong of me to pretend to be asleep because it was my turn to get up with her. But I was so darn tired.

Another cry sounded, louder this time. Mike stirred next to me, and the lamp on his nightstand switched on. I scrunched my eyes shut and tried to appear dead to the world. A futile effort since I was no actress.

Mike nudged me in the side. "I know you're awake. You can't fool me, Sal. Come on, it's your turn."

Another cry sounded, loud and impatient. Both traits ran in my family. I sighed heavily and sat up. "Fine, I'm going."

Mike's response was to roll over onto his side, and I couldn't resist adding, "Easter's this Sunday, and we've got orders coming into the bakery like crazy, you know."

He yawned sleepily into the pillow. "I do know, princess, but I have a twelve-hour day ahead of me. I've got both a furnace and a bathtub to install, plus a basement to dig through. Making cookies all day sounds like a walk in the park."

His words made me fume inwardly. I gave the pillow one final punch and stumbled out of bed.

Sensing my annoyance, Mike gave a low chuckle. I grabbed my robe from the bottom of the bed and glared at him. He opened his eyes and winked at me. I tried not to notice how good he looked in the middle of the night, his black, curly hair disheveled from sleep, plus the sexy five o'clock shadow that surrounded his sensual mouth. And those midnight blue eyes of his were always my downfall.

Waah. Waah!

The cries were becoming more insistent, and I was afraid the neighbors might hear. Spike whimpered and buried his head under the comforter as if trying to block out baby Cookie's screams. She had a fine set of lungs on her. I opened the door to her adjoining room but simply had to have the last word. "How would *you* like to stand in front of a hot oven all day? Working in a bakery is not a piece of cake, you know."

Mike laughed and closed his eyes. "Nice pun, princess. No, I never said it was easy, but it sure as hell beats standing knee deep in mud."

"Oh, whatever," I grumbled.

Cookie was clearly outraged at having been ignored for this long. The screams were almost loud enough to shake our tiny house. A sharp crunch sounded from underneath my feet as I walked across the thick, brown shag carpeting in her room. One of Cookie's rattles snapped in two, and I was grateful I'd put slippers on.

When I saw that little face in the crib looking up at me, all red and distressed, there was no way I could be upset, even though this was the third time she'd woken up tonight. I'd longed for a child for so many years and had finally gotten my wish. Cookie was both a blessing and a joy, and I thanked God for her every day. I'd thought that I'd be prepared for a child, but boy, had I been wrong. There was so much I still didn't know, but I was figuring it out as I went along.

Cookie's name was short for Corinne, my grandmother's given name. During the last month, Cookie had backtracked and gone from a decent sleep pattern of five hours to waking up after every two hours. My younger sister, Gianna, had a one-year-old boy named Alex and she'd tried to warn me. "Forget about her sleeping through the night. *You're* the one who's never going to sleep through the night again."

I'd thought she was kidding. Gianna was an attorney with a career ten times busier than my own. Running a bakery was not an easy job, but arguing a case in court when you were half asleep and had spit up on your suit had to be a heck of a lot worse.

One sniff immediately told me what was wrong. Cookie didn't smell like cookies. When I scooped her up in my arms, she rewarded me with another yell. I carried her over to the changing table and whisked off her soiled diaper as she kicked fervently in the air with her chubby legs, enjoying being uninhibited.

"My, you're always so full of energy in the middle of the night, aren't you? Can you share some with Mommy? She really needs some tonight," I crooned as I kissed the bottom of her perfect little foot. "Going out to party?"

My kiss was rewarded with a gurgling giggle. It was the cutest sound I'd ever heard. After I'd given Cookie a fresh diaper and changed her out of a green onesie into a pink sleeper, she proceeded to stuff all her fingers in her mouth. I wanted to groan. She couldn't be hungry again. Mike had given her a supplemental bottle at midnight.

I sat down in the rocker and started to nurse her. Yes, Cookie was definitely hungry. She'd weighed over ten pounds at birth and now, at four months, was up to twenty pounds. I worried she might be too heavy, but on her last visit, the doctor said both her height and weight were in the 90th percentile. He assured me that once she started crawling, she'd slim down.

I stroked Cookie's cheek and hummed a lullaby to her,

then lifted her over my shoulder to burp her, hoping she'd fall back to sleep. Not a chance. Cookie was wide awake. Ever the optimist, I tried to lay her back down in the crib, and she immediately started to cry again.

"Good night, my pretty girl," I whispered and blew her a kiss wondering who I thought I was kidding.

Even though I was back in my own room, I continued to tiptoe over to the bed and held my breath. As I settled under the covers, her cries grew louder, and I wanted to sob as well.

"For God's sake, Sal," Mike mumbled from underneath the pillow lying on top of his head. "Just bring Cookie in here and put her in bed with us."

"But I want her to get used to sleeping in her crib all night," I explained.

"Start tomorrow," Mike insisted. "I need my sleep. And so do the neighbors."

Yeah, join the club. Defeated, I sighed and went back into Cookie's room. She kept crying even after I'd picked her up, and tears of frustration trickled down my cheeks as well.

"Please. Go to sleep for Mommy," I begged. "We have an order for ten dozen lemonade cookies tomorrow and five cookie baskets to prepare."

Cookie was clearly disinterested in the bakery's plight. I laid her down between Mike and myself, and she continued to cry. I draped my arm over her head and held her against my side, but she screamed even louder. *Yikes.*

Mike rolled over to face us and reached for the baby. "Come on, my littlest princess. Daddy's here." He lifted her into his strong arms and held her against his bare, rock-hard chest, patting her back softly. Cookie started to coo and then immediately quieted. After a few minutes, he gently lowered her between us. I stared down at her in disbelief. Cookie was fast asleep, her angelic little face peaceful and content.

Mike gave me a triumphant smile. "See? She just wanted her daddy." He gave me a light kiss on the forehead, rolled back over onto his side, and immediately began snoring again.

I suppose I should have been grateful, but in truth, I was annoyed. Yes, my feelings had been hurt. Since when had Mike become the baby whisperer? With jealousy, I noted how Cookie always seemed to prefer him to me as of late. I loved the fact that she adored her father, but jeez!

I was the one who nursed Cookie, bathed her, and spent the most time with her. Three days a week she came to my bakery, Sally's Samples, where I raced between the store and the upstairs apartment all day to take care of her. One day a week she went to my sister Gianna's, where her husband, Johnny Gavelli, watched her and Alex. Johnny worked nights, so it was a great arrangement, except for the fact that he and my sister rarely saw each other.

Two days a week Cookie went to my parents' house, where my mother and grandmother both showered her with love and attention. I tried to tell myself that Cookie missed her daddy because she saw him the least amount of time. In my heart, though, I kept asking myself why Cookie was playing favorites. What was I doing wrong?

I was too tired to dissect this any further and wearily closed my eyes. I must have dozed off, because the alarm on Mike's cell went off and all three of us jerked awake in response. Mike groaned, Cookie cried, and I prayed for strength to get through this day.

"Damn it," Mike growled. "I meant to shut that off. I knew it would wake her."

I checked the clock, hoping it was wrong, but it said five thirty. Ugh. I sat up and pulled Cookie against my chest. "I feel like death warmed over."

Mike got out of bed and stretched. He still looked sexy, even half asleep, but romance was the last thing on my mind. These days, a cup of fully caffeinated coffee and sleep were my deepest desires.

Mike came around to my side of the bed and leaned down to kiss both Cookie and me. "I need the shower first. I've got to be on the road in half an hour. I'm working in Rochester today."

Rochester was over an hour away from our hometown of Colwestern, located in the Buffalo region of western New York.

Startled, I glanced up at him. "But she'll scream bloody murder while I'm in the shower."

"Sal," he protested. "If she has to cry for a few minutes,

it won't hurt her. What do you want me to do? I've got to go to work." Without another word, he walked toward the bathroom, not noticing the door was shut and stumbled into it. "Damn thing," he muttered then slammed it behind him.

Cookie was wide awake now, and the chance she'd go back to sleep before I left for work was hopeless. Thank goodness Josie was opening today. I raised myself to a sitting position and placed Cookie on my stomach facing me, her back against my raised legs. I lifted her over my head, which I knew she loved. "Is my little angel ready to spend a fun day with her Grammy and Grandpa?"

Cookie rewarded me with a giggle, gave a loud burp, and then spit up all over my face.

*   *   *

An hour and a half later, Cookie and I were on the road. I rubbed my eyes and grabbed for the travel mug in my console, taking a long swig. My daily caffeine fix was limited since Cookie was still nursing, but I had high hopes that the half caff would work its magic. I waited, but nothing happened. How could I feel like I had a hangover when I hadn't even touched alcohol in over a year?

I pulled into my parents' paved driveway and glanced into the back seat. Yes, just as I'd suspected. Cookie was fast asleep in the pink car seat, her curly black tendrils framing her sweet little face. She looked so adorable. No one who looked at her would ever dream that she could scream louder than a banshee in the middle of the night.

I hoisted the diaper bag over my shoulder and lifted the car seat then walked—no, more like teetered from side to side while making my way up the long driveway. The front door was already open, and my grandmother was waiting in the doorway. I leaned over to kiss her cheek and missed by inches.

Next to Mike and Cookie, Grandma Rosa was the other love of my life. She'd come to live with my parents when my grandfather died, shortly after Gianna was born. I'd only been three years old at the time but remembered the day well. As much as I loved my parents, Grandma Rosa had always been the one Gianna and I told all our secrets to during the stressful teen years. She never disappointed, was a wonderful listener, and gave great advice. Besides being an accomplished cook, she was also talented with both a knitting needle and crotchet hook. Above all, she was the most amazing human being I'd ever known—never judged people, was faithfully kind, and her intuition continually surprised me.

Grandma Rosa took the car seat and examined my face closely. "*Cara mia*, you look terrible. Did you get any sleep at all?"

"Not much." I checked my watch.

"Come inside for a glass of orange juice," she insisted. "The Vitamin C will help."

I shook my head. "I'm already late, Grandma, and it's not fair to Josie. She's got four kids to my one, remember."

"Bah." She nudged me inside. "Josie knows what it is like to have a new baby. The world will not end if people cannot get their cookies on time. Now come."

Without further argument, I followed her into the foyer. "Easter is this Sunday, remember. The orders are coming in like crazy."

She sniffed. "Easter should be about honoring God, not about stuffing your face with Sally Donovan's shortbread cookies. I realize that Mike and you have businesses to run, but it does more harm than good to push yourselves this hard."

Grandma Rosa set the car seat on the newly waxed linoleum floor of the kitchen while I slumped into a chair at the round oak table. There was a Pack 'n Play set up in the living room that she would place Cookie in later. A coffin had been in there until recently, but my father, who was obsessed with death in every shape and form, had moved it to my old bedroom upstairs.

I rubbed my eyes and yawned. "Cookie won't sleep through the night. She's four months old, Grandma. Josie said her kids never woke up three times during the night. Mike and I are tired and squabbling like kindergarteners."

"You need to take some time for yourselves," Grandma Rosa said thoughtfully as she handed me the juice. "Let your parents babysit while you and Mike go out and taint the town."

I winced at her choice of words. My grandmother had a bad, but adorable, habit of mixing up her phrases. "It's paint, Grandma."

"That is good too," she agreed.

"Is that my sweet granddaughter?" My mother's high heels clicked against the wooden stairs, and she appeared in the doorway. Even at this early hour, she was dressed and ready for anything. At the age of fifty-five, Maria Muccio was still a knockout, even though she'd had a bit of cosmetic surgery to help her along. Mom's hair was a tad lighter than my ebony shade, and her dark eyes, luminous and thoughtful, were framed with long lashes that reminded me of Bambi. She always wore the least amount of clothing in an attempt to show off her fabulous size-four figure.

My mother's style barely passed for decent in my eyes, but maybe I was secretly jealous because she'd always looked better than me. Even though it was only April, she was dressed in a sleeveless red mini-dress that showed off her perfect legs to their full advantage.

I put a finger to my lips. "She's sleeping, Mom. A rare commodity these days." Then again, maybe I should let my mother wake her. If Cookie stayed awake now, she'd have to sleep through the night, or at least I hoped so.

My mother bussed my cheek and filled a mug with coffee while I watched in envy. "Oh, she'll come around. Maybe she's teething. What does her pediatrician say?"

I leaned my head on my arms. "I think her doctor is starting to hate me. I call him all the time. He must think I'm the neediest mother alive."

"Baby girl? Is that you?" My father's footsteps pounded loudly on the stairs, but Cookie didn't stir. She must have been exhausted from partying all night.

I rose and put the empty glass in the sink. "Hi, Dad. I'm late and need to run."

"Come for dinner tonight," my grandmother urged. "Leave work an hour early, and then take a nap in your old room upstairs. You need it, my dear. The hags under your eyes look terrible."

Again, her choice of words made me wince, but sadly,

she wasn't far off. I did feel like a hag these days, and her offer was tempting. "I'll see how the day goes. Thanks for the juice."

"Wait a second, baby girl. I need to talk to you." My father's round and usually jovial face wore a concerned expression that caught my attention. Domenic Muccio was in his late sixties, with a head that sprouted less hair each year while his middle continued to expand. He'd retired from the railroad a few years back and since then had shifted around from careers that consisted of a hearse driver at Phibbins Mortuary, to keeping coffins in his house, and finally to running his own successful death blog. Father Death was the name he used on his blog, where he posted daily thoughts on the subject of death and funerals. To the amazement of our family, he made a decent income from the businesses that paid to advertise on his site, specifically undertakers and crematoriums.

Between the blog, his pension, and a paid-off mortgage, my mother and father lived well enough. Dad had even self-published a novel, *How to Plan and Enjoy Your Funeral,* which had gotten him a lot of attention—and ridicule—and he was currently working on another. Sure, his antics were embarrassing, but Gianna and I were convinced we must have seen it all by now.

"Can it wait until tonight? I need to get to the bakery."

Dad held up a hand. "This will only take a minute. I need your help with something, and no, it can't wait."

I tried to stifle a groan. He probably wanted to hold another book signing in the bakery and have Josie and me make our famous coffin cookies. "All right. What is it?"

My father pursed his lips. "I'm worried about Eddie Phibbins. He's missing."

Unlike my father, I didn't know Eddie well, except for the times I'd attended wakes at his funeral home. It was the most popular one in Colwestern. "What do you mean 'missing'?"

Dad stuffed his hands deep into his trouser pockets. "Eddie's my biggest client. But more importantly, he's been a good friend these past few years. Eddie always pays on time, but for the last few weeks, he's been delinquent on his account. I keep running his ads for the comfiest caskets in the world, but he hasn't paid me a red cent in return."

I'd never sampled one of Eddie's comfy coffins, so I'd have to take his word for it. "Have you talked to him about the past due invoices?"

"I shot him an email three days ago," my father explained, "and I've left several phone messages. Yesterday I finally got through to his wife, who told me that Eddie's disappeared. It's been over 48 hours since he was last seen. I was hoping you could help."

This got a laugh out of me. "Dad, I'm no detective. Has Mrs. Phibbins reported his disappearance to the police?"

My father nodded. "Yeah, Linda called them and filled out a missing persons report. But she's worried, and frankly, so am I. This isn't like Eddie. He's too responsible and devoted to his business to vanish like that. I even called the police myself and asked for your buddy Brian, but they told me he was on his honeymoon."

"Yes, he got married last week." Brian Jenkins was a police officer on the Colwestern force who I'd met when I had returned to town four years earlier, after my disastrous first marriage had ended in divorce. For a long time, Brian had been interested in me romantically, but he'd never stood a chance against Mike. I was thrilled when Brian's attention finally shifted to Ally Tetrault, a former high school classmate who'd been foaming at the mouth for him since they'd first met two years ago. "I think they're due back in a couple of days."

My father's expression was grim. "But you're a real good detective, baby girl, and have sniffed out a lot of killers. Can't you at least check into it for your old man?"

"Fool," my grandmother grunted. "Sally has a busy bakery and a baby to take care of. She has no time for your silliness. Let the police handle it."

"Dad, I'd like to help, but I don't have the experience. I just happened to be involved in a few murder cases."

He raised an eyebrow. "A *few?* Columbo has nothing on you."

Not a cheerful thought. "Sorry, Dad. I'll ask around at the bakery today, but that's the best I can do."

"Maybe he needed to get away from death for a while," my mother suggested.

My father shook his head. "No way. Eddie wouldn't do that. He loves that business more than life itself."

The irony of his words wasn't lost on us. My grandmother and I exchanged an eye roll, something she rarely did. "The police will find him soon, Dad," I assured him.

"I sure hope so, baby girl."

The look in my father's eyes unnerved me, but I tried to let it pass. "Gotta go. I'll see you tonight." I leaned down to deposit a kiss on my little girl's soft, rosy cheek. I reminded myself again how blessed I was to have her and Mike in my life, even though I worried about falling asleep on my feet today.

As I backed the car out of the driveway and just missed hitting the mailbox, Eddie's face flashed before me. I remembered the gentle and caring smile he wore whenever he shook a mourner's hand and his weary, lined face that always seemed to be grieving right along with them. He was personable and thoughtful. My father had nicknamed him Honest Eddie. The plaque outside of the funeral home read *We're here with you till the very end.* It was hard to forget that line.

A strange feeling of foreboding shot through me. For some odd reason, I sensed that the kind and gentle mortician wouldn't be returning to Colwestern anytime soon.

CHAPTER TWO

————

"Hey." Josie nudged me in the arm. "Pay attention. You're squirting frosting all over the tray. The cookies are our target, girlfriend."

I stared down at the white, gloppy mess sitting on the tray in front of me and groaned in frustration. Yes, I was a disaster in the making today, and it was becoming more and more difficult to keep my eyes open. "Sorry."

Josie stared at me in sympathy over the rim of her coffee mug. "Hang in there, hon. It will get better."

"But she won't sleep." My voice started to wobble. "I'm so tired that I want to curl up and take a nap in the oven. Is that so wrong? Oh, and I think Cookie likes Mike better than me."

Josie burst out laughing. "Where is this coming from? She's four months old, Sal. She likes whoever cuddles and feeds her. Are you giving her supplementary bottles yet?"

I nodded. "Once a day."

"Hmm." Josie frowned thoughtfully. Next to my grandmother, she was my personal expert on baby care. Josie's boys ranged from four to fourteen years old. In the four years since the bakery had opened, she'd never once taken a sick day, except for the time a lunatic had shot her. Josie was the one with the baking expertise, not me. She'd quit culinary school after one semester when she'd gotten pregnant with her eldest child. Life had thrown Josie some blows, but she'd always come up swinging.

Even after four kids, Josie still had a fantastic figure and looked younger than her 32 years. Her rich, auburn hair was pinned in a neat bun on the top of her head, and her eyes looked genuinely concerned. They always flashed blue sparks whenever she was excited or angry about something. The latter emotion was usually reserved for our assistant Dodie, an older woman who tried Josie's patience on a daily basis.

Josie knew me better than I knew myself at times, but it worked both ways. We'd been besties since the age of eight, and our friendship was as solid as steel. When Mike and I had broken up after a misunderstanding on prom night, she'd fully supported my decision but always wondered if there had been more to the situation. Josie had refused to believe that Mike had cheated on me with Brenda Snyder—aka Backseat Brenda—and it turned out that she'd been correct. Back then I'd tended to jump to conclusions, and that particular one had cost me several years of happiness before Mike and I finally found our way back to each other.

"Sal, you're a good mother. Don't beat yourself up," Josie said wisely. "This is your first baby. It gets easier with time. Trust me."

"But I need to sleep, and I can't even have caffeine. *How* is this going to get any easier?"

The silver bells on the front door jingled, and Josie stepped forward. "I've got this."

Defeated, I set the piping bag down and followed her to the storefront. Who was I kidding? I was doing more harm than good here today. Maybe I should see if Dodie could come in for the afternoon and then take a nap as my grandmother had suggested. The idea sounded more heavenly than her rich ricotta cheesecake.

Josie greeted Mrs. O'Brien, one of our more frequent customers, who was busy peering into the display case. "Hey, Mrs. O. What will it be today?"

Mrs. O'Brien bit her lower lip in concentration. "Let's see. I'll take a dozen of the jelly thumbprint cookies. Don't forget my fortune cookie, please. I need some good luck today."

Bakeries often needed a trademark to make them stand out from the competition. My novelty cookie shop was known throughout the town for the delicious varieties we made, many which were Josie's personal recipes. She also baked cakes on the side for extra income. Josie insisted on paying me for the ingredients, even though I'd argued with her, so in turn, I let her keep the entire profit. It was only fair, since she did all the work. Besides, without Josie's talent, my bakery never would have been a success.

Before I'd opened the shop, I'd come up with the idea to give out a free fortune cookie with every purchase. Fortune cookies themselves were inexpensive to make and not difficult, but they hardened quickly and often before placing the messages inside, so only a few at a time could be prepared.

"Why? Is something wrong?" I grabbed a piece of wax paper.

She made a tsk-tsk sound, but it was all for effect. Like many other Colwestern residents, Leslie O'Brien lived for gossip.

"I'm taking these to Myrna Dublin's house," she said. "Did you hear that her husband passed away? It was so sudden. The wake was last night, and there's a gathering at her house after the funeral. They should be leaving Phibbins Mortuary for the cemetery right about now."

Her casual reference to the funeral home reminded me of my promise to my father. "The wake was at Phibbins Mortuary last night?"

Mrs. O'Brien's mouth twitched in annoyance. "Yes, and what a mistake that was. They've really gone down under—err, I mean downhill."

You had to love funeral home puns. "Was Eddie there?"

"No." She crooked her finger, beckoning me to come closer. "I heard that he's skipped town."

"Why would he do that? He has a business to run," Josie said.

A broad smile crossed Mrs. O'Brien's sallow-looking face. She was in her full glory now. "Some business," she snickered. "I've heard they're on the brink of bankruptcy. I told Myrna to use End of the Road Funeral Home, but no, she wouldn't listen. She's one of those loyal types. And what did it get her? The owner didn't even show up for the wake or funeral! He left poor Linda to take care of everything, and God knows that woman is sorely lacking in the brain department."

A woman with gray, curly hair standing behind Mrs. O'Brien nodded in agreement and decided to insert her own two cents. "Suzanne Tully said she heard a rumor that Eddie was stealing from his customers. Pocketing jewelry and other things that belonged to the deceased. I never would have dreamed Eddie was capable of that. Shameful! And that fellow who was working for him—Wally something? He was stealing his urns and selling them on eBay."

Mrs. O'Brien looked disappointed with this revelation. "Really? I hadn't heard about that."

"Oh yes." The woman with gray hair heaved a sigh. "It's a grave matter, let me tell you. Ha-ha, get it?"

She and Mrs. O'Brien started to howl with laughter, but I didn't think it was funny. Now I knew why Eddie always looked sad. It wasn't the fact that he worked with dead bodies every day but the torturous puns he had to put up with.

Josie swallowed hard. "The urns on eBay. Um, they were empty, right?"

"Bless your heart, child." The woman with gray hair giggled. "Even Eddie isn't *that* cheap."

"Don't forget my fortune cookie, Sally," Mrs. O'Brien reminded me.

I reached into the case with the wax paper. The cookie was stuck to another one, so I broke them apart and it cracked in my hand. The message sprung up from the edges of the cookie as if begging me to read it.

Mrs. O'Brien watched me with interest. "Oh, no, I'll take that one." She reached out her hand. "You get the most interesting messages. It's my turn now." She gestured at the unopened cookie. "You read that one."

I handed her the cracked cookie. Interesting messages was one way to put it. When I first opened the bakery, I was convinced that the fortune cookies could predict the future. Since then I had realized it was a ridiculous notion all in my head. We usually printed our own messages, but if the bakery was too busy, like this week, we bought them by the bag from a nearby novelty store.

I listened as Mrs. O'Brien read aloud. "'A healthy mind does not speak ill of others.'"

Josie snorted back a laugh and quickly turned it into a cough.

Mrs. O'Brien glared at her then fixed her eyes on me.

"Well, that was a huge disappointment. What does yours say, Sally?"

"Mrs. O'Brien, why don't I save this one for another customer," I suggested.

She narrowed her eyes. "Be a good sport and open it up. Don't I bring you a ton of business? Didn't my son and his wife order a wedding cake from Josie? And didn't I buy a tray of cookies for the bridal shower?"

"Okay, okay." Good grief, the woman was impossible. I cracked the cookie open and stared down at the message. "Well, this is a new one. 'Live life outside of the box.'"

Mrs. O'Brien drew her eyebrows together. "You never disappoint, Sally. What do you think that means?"

My brain, like the rest of me, was half asleep, but I tried to process it anyway. "I'm guessing that you shouldn't try to confine yourself. Do as you please. Live, laugh, love." A beautiful sentiment, but something told me there was more to it.

Mrs. O'Brien waited for me to go on and looked disappointed when I didn't elaborate. "Well dear, that sounds nice, but I'm sure there must be a more ominous meaning. Something bad will happen today. I'm sure of it."

"For goodness sake," Josie sputtered. "Must you always be the customer of doom and gloom? Isn't Mrs. Gavelli bad enough?"

"Hey," Mrs. O'Brien retorted. "Don't ever compare me to Johnny's grandmother. That woman is evil. Remember, this is Sally we're talking about. Everyone in town knows that death follows her wherever she goes. Sort of like her father."

The woman with the gray hair joined her in a giggle at my expense. I bristled inwardly but said nothing. Normally I would attempt to laugh it off, but I wasn't in the mood today. I gave them both a little wave and disappeared into the back room where my cookie disaster awaited me. I began to scrape the icing off the cookies, which were supposed to be decorated like Easter eggs for a Holy Thursday celebration. Instead, they looked more like geeky, ghostly smiley faces.

The bells over the front door jingled with the women's departure, and Josie joined me a minute later. "Don't let those nosy biddies get to you, Sal."

"They think I'm a magnet for death," I complained. The last time I'd been involved in a murder was at Christmas, and I'd been nine months pregnant. Before Cookie was born, I'd promised Mike that I'd stay out of trouble and investigations, but in all fairness, it wasn't my fault. I didn't go looking for trouble or dead bodies. They just always seemed to know where to find me.

"Nah." Josie went to the three electric mixers we kept on the counter and started tossing ingredients into a metal bowl for her famous no-bake peanut butter cookies. "They're just jealous. Their lives aren't half as exciting as yours."

I gave a snort. "Mine isn't exactly anything to brag about lately. Mike and I are always tired, we argue about stupid things, and our daughter thrives on keeping us awake every night."

Josie removed her cell from her jeans pocket. "I can't believe I'm doing this, but I'm going to call Dodie to see if she can come in for the afternoon. You need to go home and get some sleep. You're not any good to the bakery like this."

Maybe I should have been insulted, but I only felt gratitude instead. "Really? You wouldn't mind?"

She gave me a sly wink. "Go home, Sal. You need it. Then call Mike to leave work early and have a little romantic interlude before you pick up Cookie."

I made a face. "That's the last thing on our minds these days."

Josie winked. "It may be the last thing on yours, but definitely not on his. Trust me. He is a man, after all."

I hung my apron on one of the metal hooks and grabbed my sweatshirt. "Okay, I'll see you tomorrow. Call me if you need anything." I started toward the back door, which led to the alley, then thought better of it. I hoisted my purse over my shoulder, hurried over to Josie's side, and crushed her with a bear hug. "Thanks, Jos."

The bells on the front door were set in motion again. Josie blew me a kiss as she left the room. "Pleasant dreams, kiddo."

The sun was shining, and for the middle of April, it was a beautiful spring day with the temperature hovering at sixty degrees. It wasn't unlikely for us to still get snow at this time of the year, but for once it seemed that spring might be right on track. Any other day I would have wanted to sit on my deck with a lemonade, enjoying the sun cascading upon my face. But today it was the thought of my warm, comfortable bed that excited me to no end.

Ten minutes later, I parked my car in the garage. I hadn't even bothered to let Mike know that I'd left work early, and guilt consumed me. It wasn't fair that I could come home and nap while he was stuck at work, but I knew he wouldn't begrudge me. When I woke up, I'd text him and ask him to meet me at my parents' for dinner.

I grabbed the mail out of the box and tossed it onto the coffee table in the living room without even looking at it. I stripped off my clothes, except for my underwear, and practically dove under the covers of the unmade bed. After a minute, I remembered my phone. I couldn't just ignore it anymore. I had a baby whose needs had to come first. I ran into the living room, grabbed it out of my purse, and set it on the nightstand.

Spike jumped onto the bed and settled himself across my feet. I knew he wanted to go for a walk, but I was too tired. Thankfully, we had the doggie door in the kitchen that he used whenever he needed to do his business. I reached down to scratch him behind the ears, murmured, "Good boy," and was out like a light.

All too soon, my dream was interrupted by an incessant buzzing. I opened my eyes and glanced at the clock. It was ten minutes after three. For a moment, I couldn't remember what day it was, and then everything came back to me. I'd been asleep for over two hours but felt even more tired than before my nap.

The buzzing mercifully stopped. Relieved, I closed my eyes again. Within seconds, it started back up, and I was sorely tempted to throw the phone out the window. I reached out my hand to the nightstand, knocked the phone to the floor, lost my balance, and fell out of bed with a thud. At least now I was awake. Cursing under my breath, I reached out to read the screen. My father's cell phone.

A wave of anxiety passed over me, as I clicked *Accept Call*. "Dad, is Cookie okay?"

"She's fine, baby girl," my father assured me. "But I'm not at the house right now."

I sat upright and stretched out my legs. I already knew what this was about. My father rarely called, unless he wanted fortune cookies or needed a favor. I tried to not let the irritation show in my voice. "Dad, I asked around about Eddie, and a few customers said he was having some financial problems. But I'm sure you'll get paid soon."

A long silence followed. "I know all about those rumors," Dad said. "People are saying he's been cheating his customers. It's terrible how your so-called 'friends' talk about you behind your back."

"Dad, I'm really tired," I pleaded. "Maybe we can talk about this when I come over to the house tonight."

"I called to tell you that I found Eddie," Dad said.

Thank goodness. I loved my father, but at the moment, I didn't have the energy to deal with him or his morbid friends. "That's great! Where is he?"

Dad cleared his throat. "In one of his coffins at the funeral home."

Bewildered, I stared at the phone. "What are you talking about? Was he sleeping?" Go figure. My father must not be the only one who liked to take the occasional nap in a coffin.

Dad's voice shook. "No. He's dead, baby girl."

CHAPTER THREE

————

My father inhaled the genetti I'd handed him in one gulp. The Italian cookies with sugary icing and nonpareils were his favorite, besides the bakery's fortune cookies, that is. I was glad that I'd thought to bring some with me. In desperate situations like this, my father's first thought always turned to food.

I placed a hand on his arm. "Dad, you're not making any sense. Did Eddie become sick and collapse inside the coffin?"

Dad shook his head and reached for another cookie. "I don't think so. He was fit as a fiddle. That man had a lot of life left in him."

His words echoed through the empty viewing room of Phibbins Mortuary. After my father's startling phone call, I'd quickly gotten dressed and driven over with the cookies in tow to be with him. There was nothing we could do for poor Eddie now but my father had wanted me here, and I couldn't say no.

Almost as distressing as learning that Eddie had been found dead in one of his coffins was to see my father in this present state of mind. He always had such an optimistic look on life—or death, for that matter.

The coroner was currently in the display room, where Eddie had been found, located at the rear of the building. An officer from Colwestern's police force who I didn't recognize was with him. The man looked like he was barely out of high school and must have been a new trainee. Thanks to my history of finding dead bodies, I knew almost everyone in the department. Two EMTs had also been present but had departed once the coroner had arrived. There was nothing that they could do for poor Eddie either.

My father peered into the bakery bag sitting between us.

"Got any fortune cookies in there?"

I reached into the bottom of the bag and handed him one. Between Dad and Mrs. Gavelli, someone in my life always needed a fortune cookie, so I'd learned to be prepared. "Dad, don't you think we've run out of good luck for today?"

"We'll keep it for tomorrow, then." Dad cracked the cookie open and read the message silently to himself. "Huh. Any other day I'd consider this a great omen, but my heart's not in it right now."

I peered over his shoulder and read the strip of paper. *Look alive. You never know what tomorrow will bring.*

Good grief. I snatched the message out of his hands. "Forget you even saw that, Dad."

He sighed heavily. "To top it all off, you know what those monsters did to him? They put him in a pine box. *A pine box!* The man deserved at least bronze. If that isn't a slap in the face, I don't know what is."

I stared at him in disbelief. "He's dead, Dad. That's about the worst thing that can happen to him."

"You don't understand, baby girl." He put his head in his hands as if it ached. "It was just the icing on the cake, err, casket, so to speak."

"Not funny, Dad."

Irritated, he threw up his hands. "I'm not trying to be funny. Eddie would be mortified if he knew. It's an embarrassment to his profession. Pine boxes are the cheapest type of coffins they make." His expression was solemn. "Take the clasps on the outside of the coffin, for instance. They're flimsy, just like the rest of it. When I bought mine, I checked some of the other models out. I was crazy enough to even sample a pine one. The lid closed on me while I was inside, and the lock snapped shut in place. It was no big deal. I was able to get out easy enough."

"Don't, Dad. No more."

He sighed. "Who could have done this to such a fine, upstanding man?"

"That's what I'd like to know too."

The familiar male voice drew my attention, and I turned around to meet Brian Jenkins' gaze. He was standing in the doorway watching my father and me. He looked different from the last time I'd seen him about three weeks ago. Brian had stopped by the bakery for some chocolate chip cookies a few days before his wedding. Of course, I'd given him a dozen on the house.

The surprise on my face must have shown because he shot me a full-fledged grin. Although he'd always been handsome with that Greek godlike profile of his, Brian looked even better today. His dirty blond hair was a shade lighter than I remembered and most likely due to relaxing on a tropical island. His brilliant green eyes shimmered in the overhead light, while his skin had a healthy glow to it. Marriage obviously agreed with him, and I was glad.

"Congratulations." I smiled in return. "How was Aruba?"

Brian's white teeth gleamed when he smiled. "It was great, thanks. The only bad thing was that we had to come back."

"I thought you weren't returning for a couple of more days," I said.

Brian strode over to us. "We got back yesterday. I wasn't supposed to return to work until tomorrow, but when I heard the name Muccio over the police radio, let's just say that curiosity got the best of me."

"Hilarious," I muttered.

Brian placed his hands on his hips and eyed my father sharply. "What were you doing here by yourself, Domenic, and why were you looking inside coffins?"

A loaded question for sure.

"Hey," my father protested. "I didn't do anything wrong. Eddie gave me a key a while back. He said I was welcome to stop by and try out one of his models whenever I felt like it. So I started checking the merchandise out."

Brian's jaw dropped. "You mean you were looking to take a nap in it?"

"Well, not that particular model," Dad said. "Too cheaply made. But most of them are really comfortable, son. You should try one out sometime."

Brian looked like someone was playing a cruel joke on him. "Thanks, but I'll pass. What about the alarm? How'd you shut it off?"

"Eddie gave me the code a while back. Piece of cake to remember since his birthday is the Fourth of July. Seven—"

Brian interrupted him with a wave of his hand and then wrote something on the electronic tablet he was holding. I was amazed to see that our police department was becoming modernized. From what I knew, their budget was almost nonexistent.

He addressed my father again. "You opened the lid, and there he was?"

My father blew out a shaky breath. "Yes."

I squeezed his hand. "It's okay. Take your time, Dad."

"You're usually more talkative than this, Domenic." Brian's eyes clouded over with suspicion. "What gives?"

I stared at him in disbelief. "He already gave a statement to your coworker. My father's in shock, Brian. It's not every day that you find your friend dead inside a coffin."

Dad reached for another cookie. "It's all right, baby girl." He paused for a second, his eyes darting from me to Brian. "Do you want to know what the worst part was?"

"You mean there's more? Something worse than finding him dead in a pine box?" I asked.

Dad's face was ashen. "He'd already been embalmed," he whispered. "Eddie was all ready for his trip to the big funeral parlor in the sky."

Ew. He hadn't told me this part yet. "You mean that someone killed him and then did all the necessary preparations for—" Oh, this was too much. My stomach started to churn until I thought I might be sick. "What kind of a lunatic are we talking about?"

Brian's healthy-looking tan was fading fast. He put his head down and typed some more notes into the tablet. "It must have been someone who worked here." He jerked his finger in the direction of the viewing room. "Who's in there with the coroner?"

"Not Adam," my father said, referencing Brian's partner. "Some guy with carrot-colored hair."

"That's Keith. He's new to the force." Brian stuck the tablet under his arm. "Excuse me for a second, I'll be right back. Don't go anywhere."

I groaned and checked my watch again. It was almost six o'clock. "I'd better text Mike and tell him what's going on."

A sharp, piercing wail filled the building, and I clutched at my father's arm. "What the heck was that? It sounded like a wild animal."

"Nah." Dad was clearly unruffled. "Linda must be here. I'd know that voice anywhere."

"Don't you like Mrs. Phibbins?" I asked curiously.

"Oh, Linda's all right," Dad said. "But she's never been a fan of the funeral home. You see, Eddie's dad left the place to him when he died. His younger brother Arthur was furious because he'd always wanted the business." He glanced around the room in awe. "I mean, who could blame him? The place is a gold mine. You're always going to have customers."

Boy was that the truth.

Brian came back into the room leading a woman by the elbow. I'd never met Linda Phibbins before. Like her husband, she was in her early sixties but appeared much older. She was rail thin, with cropped dark hair that had a healthy dose of gray mixed in, sunken cheeks, and a wide, flat nose.

My father rose to his feet and held out a hand to her. "Linda. How are you, dear?"

"Oh, Domenic." She wept softly into a starched white handkerchief. "I just can't believe this has happened. Officer Jenkins said you're the one who found Eddie? But how? I don't understand."

"Eddie gave me a key a while back," he explained.

She looked confused. "I didn't realize. Oh well, it doesn't really matter." She sank heavily into the chair next to his. "Nothing matters anymore."

My father stared up at Brian. "Any idea of what killed him?"

"Not yet." Brian's mouth twisted into a frown. "An autopsy will be performed but since he's been embalmed already, it could interfere with toxicology results."

Tears ran down Linda's cheeks, making her age spots more prominent, and my heart filled with sorrow for her. I knew from my father that they'd been married for over thirty years. "Can I get you anything, Mrs. Phibbins?" I asked. "Some water perhaps?"

Linda seemed to see me for the first time. "Are you with the police department too?"

"No, but she should be," my father said proudly. "Linda, this is my daughter, Sally Donovan. I don't think you two have ever met."

"Oh, of course." She reached out to take my hand in her tiny one and I managed to hold back a yelp. It was like touching an ice cube. "Nice to meet you, dear. You're the one who makes the coffin cookies, correct? Eddie just loved them."

I tried to smile. Of all the delicious cookies Josie and I baked, over 20 varieties, it was the fortune and coffin cookies we were known for, which I still found strange at times. "Yes, that's right."

"Never mind the cookies," Dad interrupted. "I mean, they are pretty awesome, but Sal has other talents. She's solved more murders than the police department. She'll find out what happened to Eddie. I'd stake my own life on it."

CHAPTER FOUR

———

A muscle ticked in Brian's jaw. "Don't you think you're exaggerating a bit, Domenic?"

"Nope." My father gazed at me with pride. "Sal will find Eddie's killer, mark my words. She's like a dog with a bone when it comes to sniffing out death." He puffed out his chest. "She gets it from her old man."

My face began to warm. "Uh, Dad, you're giving me way too much credit. Sure, I've helped with a few cases, but I'm no detective."

He acted as if he hadn't heard me. "Linda, I think it would be a good idea for Sal to ask your employees some questions."

"Excuse me." Brian's voice was tinged with annoyance. "If it's all right with you, Domenic—and Sally—I'll ask the questions. Mrs. Phibbins, who else here did embalming besides your husband?"

"Everyone who works here knows the process," Linda said. "Eddie made sure that all the employees were properly trained."

"Even yourself?" Brian asked.

She hung her head. "No. Eddie wanted me to learn, but I refused." She glanced from Brian to my father and me then shut her eyes as if grasping for the right words. "I'm afraid I haven't always been as supportive of the funeral home as I should have. It was Eddie's passion, not mine. I helped with accounting sometimes or answered phones, but that's about it. It just wasn't my cup of tea."

"Not everyone has the talent or stomach for it," my father added.

Linda shot him a surly look and continued. "Eddie once told me that I was a coward. But I can't help it. Death isn't in my blood."

I couldn't believe that I was sitting here listening to this conversation, and apparently, neither could Brian. His mouth opened and then shut in a robotic manner. After a few seconds, he cleared his throat and tried again. "Who are your other employees? We'll need to get a hold of them and question everyone."

Linda blew her nose into the handkerchief. "It's a small staff. There's Zach Stevens, our doorman. He was driving the hearse up until last year, but his eyesight isn't that great anymore. When Wally was hired as a driver, Eddie had Zach change to doorman, which he wasn't very happy about. As for myself, I stay behind and make conversation with mourners who don't take the trip to the cemetery. People like to linger, you know."

"Anyone else?" Brian asked.

"Charlene Jones, our cosmetologist, and Wally Watson, who I already mentioned." She stared down at her hands. "He's not here anymore."

"You mean he's dead?" I asked.

Linda gave a bitter laugh. "Don't I wish."

My father snorted. "Eddie told me all about that scam artist, Linda. He had some nerve."

"Perhaps one of you would care to enlighten me," Brian said calmly.

Linda held up a hand before my father could continue. "Wally worked as a part-time driver for us," she explained. "When Eddie caught him stealing, he fired him." Her nostrils flared. "He was selling our urns on eBay. Can you believe it?"

"They weren't already used, were they?" my father asked. "I mean, that would be in extremely bad taste."

I shifted in my seat uncomfortably. If you asked me, this entire conversation was in bad taste.

"The name is familiar," Brian remarked. "I think he may have been arrested right before I went on vacation."

"Oh yes." Linda nodded. "Eddie was so upset that he pressed charges. Wally tried to claim that we'd never paid him and that Eddie said he could take the urns in exchange. His wife was so mortified that she left him shortly afterwards. Wally put Eddie through hell."

"So where is Wally now?" I asked, ignoring Brian's frown.

"He's out on bail, awaiting trial. The man is pure evil. He even accused Eddie of flirting with his wife. The whole thing was just ridiculous," she huffed.

Brian looked up from his tablet. "Were there any other women interested in your husband that way, Mrs. Phibbins?"

She looked at Brian as if he had corn growing out of his ears. "Are you kidding? He had many admirers. Eddie was handsome as all get out."

Brian cocked an eyebrow but didn't reply. We all knew that Linda was stretching the truth a bit. Mom often compared my father to George Clooney, so it was possible that both she and Linda were infatuated with their spouses. Looks weren't everything, and inside a person was what really counted. Nevertheless, Eddie had been lacking a bit in the George Clooney department, with his long, angular face, and enormous, pear-shaped ears that contained more hair inside them than on top of his actual head. Sadly, the only famous George that Eddie resembled was Curious George.

"A great man," my father said in a husky voice. "He'd do anything for a person in need. Why, there was a woman who couldn't pay for her mother's funeral last year. He knew she didn't have the money and told her to give him what she could afford. Remember, Linda?"

She let out a sob and nodded. "Oh my, yes. She never did pay the entire sum. That wasn't the only time it happened, either. Eddie got stiffed many times."

I held my breath, afraid someone might laugh, but fortunately no one did.

"I'll stop and have a chat with Wally." Brian stuck the tablet under his arm again. "Mrs. Phibbins, can I trouble you for phone numbers of the other employees?"

She sniffed again. "Of course, Officer."

Brian watched her anxiously. "Is there someone you can call to stay with you? A family member? Friends? Children?"

She shook her head. "Our only son, Terry, lives in

London. I'll call him, of course, but he and Eddie weren't very close." She wiped her eyes. "He was embarrassed that his father was an undertaker. Like me, he never understood the business. I doubt he'll even come for the funeral."

Tears gathered in my eyes. "I'm so sorry."

Linda gave me a rueful smile as she rose to her feet. "I'll get that information for you, Officer." She hesitated. "But there is someone else you should be questioning. Eddie's brother, Arthur."

"Does he work here too?" Brian asked.

Linda's wide mouth, lined generously with a dark shade of purple lipstick, hardened. "No, but he'd like to. He's always been furious that the funeral home was left to Eddie instead of him."

Someone with a surefire motive to want Eddie dead. Now we were getting somewhere.

We all waited for Linda to continue, but my father interrupted, stroking his chin thoughtfully. "I met Arthur once. He came in here and tried to start a fight with Eddie. You don't think—"

"Does he know how to embalm a body?" Brian cut in.

"Yes, of course," Linda said. "The funeral home has been in the family for decades. Their father, Horace Phibbins, started the place. Arthur and Eddie worked here since they were teenagers. Shortly before Horace's death, he and Arthur had a terrible argument. Horace changed his will, and Eddie was the only one to inherit the place. Arthur almost went crazy. He contested the will, but in the end, the funeral parlor still went to Eddie."

"How long ago was this?" Brian asked.

Linda twisted her hands together. "About four years ago."

"Hey, Brian." The police officer with the carrot-colored hair appeared in the doorway. "The coroner wants to have a word with you. He's still in the display room."

Brian nodded. "Be right there, Keith. Excuse me for a second, folks."

After Brian left the room, Linda hiccupped back a sob. "I don't know what I'm going to do, Domenic. Business has been slow, and Eddie always took charge of everything. I don't have a clue as to how to manage the place."

My father patted her hand. "Don't worry. Business will pop back up. I mean, look on the bright side, Linda. You're always going to have customers."

He had such a way with words.

Dad snapped his fingers. "I have an idea. Since we have the best detective in town sitting right here in this room, Eddie's murder will be easy to solve."

"*You?*" Linda's tone was incredulous.

"Aw, shucks." Dad blushed. "Nice of you to say, but my talents lie elsewhere."

"He's referring to his blog and writing books," I said hurriedly, hoping Linda wouldn't get the wrong idea.

"Like I said, Sal is top notch. Don't let her modesty fool you. Give her a chance to crack the case."

Linda looked unimpressed. "Did she catch someone stealing cookies in her shop?"

The sarcasm in her tone wasn't lost on me, but I refrained from comment. What good would it do? The woman was grieving, after all. Besides, I didn't want to become involved in Eddie's murder case.

"That's kid's stuff," Dad laughed. "Sal's solved murders. Real *Forensic Files* type of stuff. Let's see, when her ex got murdered, she found the killer before the police did. Then there was her ex's lover who died after eating Sal's cookies, and she tracked down her killer too. And we can't forget the Mafia guy who died in her bakery when it burned down, or the old woman who was stealing Josie's recipes and got mowed over by a car—"

Good grief. This was embarrassing and not exactly an endorsement for my bakery. "Dad, that's probably enough details."

My father's eyes took on a sudden, faraway gleam. It was the same look he got whenever a new idea struck him. "Linda, don't you have gatherings in your private room after a wake or funeral?"

She nodded. "Sometimes. We always offer the room at an extra charge with our funeral packages. Many people find it's a money saver, instead of holding a separate reception in a restaurant. I buy cookies and coffee. If the family wants a more elaborate menu, they can have it catered."

"Hmm." My father was deep in thought. "What if Sal and Josie provide the cookies after your next wake? Sal could bring some of her coffin and fortune cookies too."

Was he kidding? "No, Dad," I said in exasperation.

To my chagrin, Linda seemed interested. "Fortune and coffin cookies at a reception. They might get some special interest."

Oh, this was a bad idea.

"Sure they would." Dad looked pleased with himself. "Sal and Josie could cater the event. Josie's the real baker, but Sal does try hard."

I struggled not to roll my eyes. "Gee, thanks."

"The coffin cookies would go like hotcakes," Dad assured Linda. "You could probably up your price for the reception if you told your clients about them. Why, they're the bomb."

Linda sniffed. "Eddie loved those cookies so."

"While Sal's there, she could ask questions and do some investigating into Eddie's death," my father continued. "That way your employees wouldn't suspect a thing."

I glanced uneasily around the room. "Dad, the police are perfectly capable of finding Eddie's killer without my help."

"Sure, they are," he agreed. "But what harm would it to do poke around a bit? What do you think, Linda?"

What about what I thought?

Linda sighed and rose to her feet. "Sure, Domenic, it's fine. As a matter of fact, there's a wake and reception scheduled tomorrow night for Evelyn Peacock. Her family has requested the room to save money."

"No kidding," my father mused. "I hadn't heard that she died. Poor old broad."

"Dad!"

My father colored. "Sorry. I didn't mean to sound disrespectful."

Evelyn Peacock and her husband Lawrence had run Peacock's Dry Cleaning for the past forty years. It was one of the oldest businesses in town. The Peacock family lived by the famous motto, *Cleanliness is next to Godliness* for their business, while Colwestern had adopted the appropriate, *Don't Ruffle a Peacock's Feathers* in their honor.

"It's all right," Linda said. "She *was* an old broad. Meaner than a snake and full of venom. With all the money that family has, can you believe her skinflint husband asked if we had any display caskets he could get for half price? And he only wants cookies, cake, and coffee at the reception."

"What a cheapskate." My father shook his head in dismay.

Linda turned to me. "If you could come in around six or six thirty to set up, that would be great."

I stared at Linda in amazement. "You mean you're still open for business?"

"We have no choice. There's a public to serve. As Eddie always said, the show must go on."

My father gave a sad smile. "He had such a way with words."

"What about the funeral?" I asked. "Will they have a reception after that too?"

"Mr. Peacock's having a small affair at his house after the funeral," Linda replied. "He thinks more people will come to the wake. The wake probably won't wind down until after nine o'clock."

"I can't stay that late," I blurted out.

"It's fine," Linda said. "You and your partner can come by and drop off the cookies whenever you get a chance. I'll pay you for them, and then you can do whatever you like—as far as questioning people, that is." She rose. "Excuse me, but I need to get some air."

After she'd left the room, I turned on my father in annoyance. "Dad, you've done some strange things before, but this one takes the cake. People might be offended by coffin cookies at a gathering. Think about it. You're mourning a loved one, and then someone offers you a cookie shaped like a coffin?"

He gave my hair an affectionate tug. "That's where you're wrong, baby girl. People like to eat. Colwestern recently voted in a nationwide poll that dessert was their favorite meal. This town lives for gossip—and funerals." Dad chuckled. "Hey, I think I just made a funny."

"But it's *not* funny," I insisted. "And I don't have time."

"Just for one night," my father pleaded. "Sal, Eddie was a good man. Linda's a nice lady, but she's never been the sharpest crayon in the box. I realize the police are competent, but the department's overloaded. Keith told me so himself. We need someone who cares enough about Eddie to help, and I can't do it alone." He stared at me in earnest. "I have faith in you, baby girl."

My father always knew what buttons to push with me. "I still don't think this is a very good idea. Mike has to work late tomorrow night, so what am I going to do about Cookie? I am *not* bringing her here."

"You and Josie can stop over after work. Come by the house for a bite to eat. Your mother and I will watch the baby. Two hours out of your life, and who knows what might happen? You might end up solving the murder and get great exposure for the bakery. It wouldn't surprise me one bit."

I hesitated. While I didn't want to disappoint my father, I was starting to feel a bit overwhelmed by all the responsibilities in my life. "All right, one night and that's it. I want to help, Dad, but I have a bakery to run and a baby to care for." And a husband I never spent time with anymore, but I didn't say that out loud.

Dad looked pleased. "That's great. It's all going to work out fine, trust me. I have every confidence in you." He shoved another cookie into his mouth. "You and Josie will make some money and help Linda out in the process. One hand washes the other."

"I promised Mike when Cookie was born that I'd stay away from sleuthing."

"You can't stay away," Dad insisted. "It's always going to be a part of you. Don't you realize that by now?"

His statement was bothersome but fairly accurate. Since my return to Colwestern almost four years ago, I'd been involved in more murder investigations that I cared to count. My grandmother had once told me that it might be my destiny.

"Don't worry," Dad said with his usual cheeriness. "Mike will understand. He's a good man."

"All right," I gave in wearily. "Josie and I will be here."

Heck, it was only one night out of my life. What was the worst thing that could happen?

CHAPTER FIVE

———

Josie shook her head in disbelief as she assembled coffin cookies on the table in front of us. "This is nuts. I can't believe I'm going to bring coffin cookies to a wake. Does your father stay awake at night thinking up these crazy ideas?"

I looked up from the tray of fortune cookies that I was inserting messages into. "I couldn't say no, Jos. It means so much to him."

Josie eyed me with curiosity as she decorated the chocolate-frosted lids with a white cross. "What I really want to know is what Mike said. He thought your sleuthing career was over when you had Cookie."

I squirmed under her gaze. "He doesn't know—yet."

"Are *you* crazy?" she asked. "I hope you're not planning to wait until you're at the funeral parlor to call him."

The thought *had* crossed my mind, but I knew Mike would become even more upset if I waited until the last minute.

"Hey, I didn't plan this." My tone sounded defensive. "I was asleep when he got home last night, and he left before Cookie and I were up this morning." At least before I was fully awake. "We didn't get a chance to talk." This was the new norm for us these days. I'd go to bed when Cookie fell asleep, Mike would give her a supplemental bottle when he got home, and then I'd get up with her when she woke again. Last night she'd been up three times.

Josie's face was sympathetic. "Sal, you don't need this extra hassle. Plus, what happens when Brian finds out you're conducting your own investigation? Did you happen to think he might be at the wake tonight? He won't be happy either."

"I'm used to that. But why would Brian be at Mrs.

Peacock's wake?"

Josie moved the cookies to a silver tray. "Because it's going to be a mob scene. And I'm not talking about mourners for Evelyn. No one liked that sour puss."

The Peacocks did impeccable garment cleaning, but the family itself had never been overly friendly in our community and always kept to themselves.

"That's a terrible thing to say! She's been ill for the last couple of years. Maybe that had to do with her temperament."

"You know that's not true," Josie snorted. "She was never in the best temperament. Don't you remember that time when we trick-or-treated at their house, and she chased us off her porch with a broom? She told us to go beg for candy somewhere else."

"I'd forgotten about that."

Josie went on. "Or what about the day she came into the bakery after it had just opened and told us that she should get a senior citizen discount every day of the week, not just on Tuesdays? Let's not forget about the time her grandson Kevin took me to the school dance and got in trouble for drinking alcohol. She tried to blame the entire episode on me, and I was stone-cold sober."

"It might have been the only dance where you were sober," I teased.

Josie placed her hands on her slim hips. "That's true. Anyhow, I'm sorry the woman is dead, but this isn't about her. People are going to be at the funeral home because of Eddie. This is the first wake to be held since his death was announced, so maybe mourners think they're getting a two for one show."

"Then they're in for a rude awakening," I said. "Dad called earlier to tell me Eddie will be buried in a private ceremony. They have to wait until after the autopsy is conducted, of course, and other tests must be done. He said Linda's not even going to let their employees attend."

Josie covered the tray of coffin cookies with plastic wrap. "Everyone in town's already guessing about what happened to him. It's the biggest thing that's happened to Colwestern since you got carjacked by Santa Claus."

Why did I always have to be at the center of our town's

weirdness?

Josie put the frosting bowl in the sink. "When you were on the phone earlier with your grandmother, a couple of customers came in and were talking about Linda. They think she's the one who offed Eddie."

"Oh, for goodness sake," I protested.

Josie pointed the frosting knife at me. "Hey, you and I have learned the hard way that anyone is capable of murder."

"But what good would his death do her? Linda would inherit the funeral home and its financial problems. She said she has no idea how to run the place."

"Then I'm betting on one of their employees," Josie said. "Maybe that Wally guy who stole Eddie's urns. What do you think?"

I carefully covered the chocolate fudge cake Josie had made for the reception tonight. "Honestly, I don't know what to think, but I'd like to find out more about Arthur Phibbins. He wanted that funeral home and, according to Linda, would do anything to get his hands on it."

"He won't be allowed at the private service for Eddie? His own brother?" Josie asked.

"Don't think so. Dad said that Linda didn't want him there. Apparently, he's been harassing her with phone messages. She's thinking about getting a restraining order against him."

Josie snorted. "I bet you five bucks he shows up tonight." She stared down at the rows of coffin cookies in front of her. "At least we have the food situation covered. I made two hundred cookies and baked a strawberry cake for a backup if needed. If there's another reception tomorrow, I can make more coffin cookies. Dodie will be in to help."

"No way. I already told my father we're not doing this again."

Josie took the tray of fortune cookies I'd assembled. "Fine with me. But we're still going to make a very nice profit from the Peacocks' shindig."

"This just seems in such poor taste," I sighed. "I don't want to be known as a funeral vendor."

Josie started toward the display case. "This is Colwestern, Sal. The tackier, the better. When are you going to tell Mike, by the way?"

"I'll call him shortly. He won't be upset because he has to work late anyway, and my parents are fine with me leaving Cookie with them. I'll let Mike know that we're catering an event." Hey, it wasn't a total lie.

"Well, well," Josie called out. "Looks like you're going to get your chance sooner than you planned."

"What are you talking about?" I wiped my hands on my apron and joined her by the display case. Sure enough, a navy blue truck was parked at the side of the road. I watched as my husband alighted from it, looking his usual handsome and rugged self in dark blue jeans, matching jean jacket, and work boots.

I crossed over to the front door as he pushed it open. He grinned and placed his arms around me. "Hey, beautiful. I was coming in here for cookies but figured I'd see if there were any gorgeous women hanging around."

"It must be your lucky day since there's two of us," Josie called out.

He grinned at her then cupped my face between his hands and pressed his mouth against mine. "Mm. Tastes like cinnamon."

I gave him a sheepish look. "Okay, I may have had a snickerdoodle."

"Or four," Josie called out.

I ran my hands over his chest. "This is a nice surprise. What are you doing here?"

Mike gazed into my eyes with a smile that made my heart melt. "I finished the Shelby roof earlier than I thought. I'd planned to start on the Gardners' kitchen, but they won't be ready for me until tomorrow, so I have the rest of the day free." He kissed me again, more passionately this time, and for a few seconds I forgot where I was.

Josie cleared her throat. "Good thing there's no customers, or they'd be in full gawk mode. Excuse me, lovebirds. I'll be in the back room. Someone has to keep this bakery running."

I pulled my mouth away from Mike's and called out, "I'll be back there in a second to help."

Mike's face shone with excitement. "You look

exhausted, princess. I thought I'd go home, grab a quick nap, then get some takeout for us. When you get done for the day, we can have some alone time before we pick up Cookie. If she wakes up tonight, I'll take care of her." He pressed his lips against my ear and whispered, "It's been a while, baby."

His voice was low and seductive, his message clear. Desire and disappointment stirred in the pit of my stomach. I hadn't been fully on board for the wake and reception tonight, and now I regretted it even more. At this rate, Mike and I probably wouldn't have another chance to relax and enjoy each other's company until Sunday after the Easter celebration. He needed to have the kitchen done soon, and that would mean more late nights for him. By the end of the week, the bakery would be standing room only as everyone came in for their holiday treats.

I bit into my lower lip. "It sounds wonderful, but I'm going to be a little later than I thought."

A frown creased his face. "Why? What's going on?"

"Josie and I agreed to go to Phibbins Mortuary tonight. We'll be catering a reception there and bringing cookies and cake. It won't be much work, and we'll make a killing." I shuddered and put a hand to my mouth. "Oh wow. I didn't mean that the way it sounded."

Mike didn't laugh. His midnight blue eyes searched mine questioningly. "Why do I feel there's something else going on that you're not telling me?"

I wound a strand of hair around my finger. "I'm not sure what you mean."

He reached out to grab my left hand in his right one. "You're twisting your hair. That's never a good sign. I can tell when you're keeping something from me. If I had to wrangle a guess, it has to do with Eddie Phibbins' murder."

I exhaled sharply. "My father thought it would be a good way to help her out and turn a nice profit at the same time. We don't have to wait on people. Once Linda pays us, Josie and I can—"

Mike stared at me in disbelief. "So, the mourners are going to be eating coffin cookies after the wake? That's insane. Then again, anything goes around here."

I gave him a peck on the lips. "If all goes well, we'll be

home long before the wake ends."

Mike's gaze didn't waver from my face. "Tell me the truth, Sal. Your father asked you to check into that guy's death, didn't he?"

I hesitated a second too long. "Yes, but—"

He cut me off. "I thought we agreed that your sleuthing days were over when you became a mother. It's too dangerous. You've almost gotten yourself killed multiple times, even when you were pregnant. Or have you forgotten about that already?"

My jaw almost hit the floor. "Of course I haven't forgotten. You told me back then that it wasn't my fault—only bad luck. I was in the wrong place at the wrong time."

His mouth hardened. "You're *always* in the wrong place at the wrong time, which is why I don't want you going there tonight. No, Sal. I won't have you putting your life in danger to find out who killed your father's friend. Let the police handle it. That's what they get paid for."

"But I promised my father I would be there. I'm not doing any real detective work. I can't go back on my word now."

Mike sighed and released me. "I really hate this. We have a daughter to think about. You can't keep doing this. It's like you have some death wish constantly hanging over your head. If Josie wants to go, that's her business, but I'd hope you'd respect my wishes and tell your father you can't make it."

His words crushed me to the core. "Please don't be upset. You know I'd rather be home with you and Cookie. It's only for one night, okay?"

Mike looked at me sadly then leaned down to give me a peck on the lips. "I wish I could believe that, Sal, but something tells me it won't be the case." He pushed the door open, then turned to face me one last time. "We'll miss you tonight."

My heart started to break in two as I watched Mike make his way to the truck. I ran to the window, but he didn't even glance my way. Within seconds, he'd driven away from the curb, tires squealing, while I attempted to blink back tears.

Josie came out of the back room and put an arm around my shoulders. "I heard the whole thing. He didn't take it well, huh?"

"That's an understatement." I drew a hand across my

eyes.

She gave my arm a squeeze. "What do you want to do? Should we still be going through with it? I can go to the funeral home without you."

I stared out into the street again, but Mike's truck was long gone. "No, I promised to be there. We'll ask a few questions and probably won't learn anything. I'll make it up to Mike when I get home."

"Are you sure?" she asked gently.

"Positive." I smiled, thinking of the sexy, red silk nightgown he'd bought me for Valentine's Day that I hadn't even had a chance to wear yet. "When I get home, everything will be fine. You'll see."

Josie shot me a doubtful look but said nothing.

CHAPTER SIX

———

"Holy cow," Josie muttered under her breath. "I don't think I've ever seen so many people at a wake before."

We were standing in the hallway, next to the private room's entrance. Mourners were proceeding into the funeral home at a rapid pace, and we had a perfect view every time the front door opened.

Phibbins Mortuary had two "slumber" rooms, as my father called them, with a folding wall in between. Tonight, the wall had been rolled back in order to accommodate the mob scene–sized crowd.

Josie and I had arrived at six thirty, after closing the bakery for the night. My car needed some exhaust work so she'd followed me over to the local garage first so I could drop it off. We usually closed the bakery at five, but when there were holidays involved, we stayed open until six o'clock.

There were familiar townspeople who smiled at us but then whispered amongst themselves. I'd developed quite a reputation in Colwestern over the years. Since I was frequently featured in the local newspaper, my bakery was often referred to as Sally's Shambles instead of Sally's Samples.

I peered out the nearby window. "This is insane. The line is wrapped around the block. There must be at least a hundred people outside."

Josie tapped her foot impatiently and went to peer into the viewing room again. She came back seconds later, her lips drawn tight. "I know that Linda saw us. Can't she break away from the mourners for a minute to come and pay us?"

We'd been waiting for almost an hour, and I'd promised Mike I wouldn't be long. We were having enough problems already, and here I was adding to them. Lack of sleep, lack of romance, and now he felt like he couldn't trust me. What a great basis for a marriage. "Well, while we're stuck here, I might as well talk to some of the employees. Do you think we can get a word with the doorman?"

"I don't know. He's doing a booming business," Josie declared. "His name is Zach, right? What do you make of him? He looks like he needs a coffin himself."

"Jos!"

She looked sheepish. "Well, he has to be in his eighties at least."

"It's a shame he's still working at that age," I said pityingly. "Unless he enjoys it."

Josie looked at me like I had two heads. "Apart from your father, who else would enjoy anything about this business?"

"Eddie seemed to like it," I said.

She snorted. "Yeah and look where that got him."

Zach was opening the door and allowing a few people in at a time. The entranceway and viewing room were filled to capacity with every kind of flower imaginable. A small table with a vase of orchids was to our left, and one of lilies and white roses was to our right. I usually loved the scent, but they were overpowering, and Josie and I were doing our best to keep from sneezing. The delicious scent of the coffee we'd made earlier drifted over from the private room and helped sustain me. We'd already set our goodies up in there too.

"That coffee smells so good," I sighed. "I'm dying for a cup."

"Those puns just keep coming," Josie teased.

Ouch. "I didn't mean it the way it sounded."

A shrill, stubborn female voice caught our attention. "Let me in. I no wait."

"Hey, she cut the line!" a man yelled.

"You let me in," the woman demanded.

"By every hair of her chinny chin chin," Josie whispered. "Yep, it's either the Big Bad Wolf or Mrs. Gavelli."

Frankly, I would have preferred the wolf. The voice rambled on, but this time in Italian, and moments later, a tiny woman dressed in black pushed her way past Zach and into our line of vision. Nicoletta Gavelli had lived next door to my parents for thirty years. She'd raised Johnny, her grandson and Gianna's husband, from the age of five when his mother, Nicoletta's only daughter, had died of a drug overdose.

Nicoletta and I had a love-hate relationship at times—but she did with most people. My grandmother was the only person who wasn't afraid to stand up to her. Johnny and I had been friends since childhood, and she'd once caught us in a compromising position in her garage playing "doctor." I'd only been six years old and the entire game had been Johnny's idea, but Nicoletta refused to believe her grandson was at fault. To this day, she still didn't trust me and claimed I was always up to no good.

"Nicoletta," Zach said to her politely. "You can't butt the line."

"Bah, what you say." She waved an irritated hand in his direction. Her eyes, dark as coal, caught sight of Josie and me. Uh-oh. I hoped she wouldn't make a scene.

"Aha!" she said, triumph registering in her voice as she hurried toward us. "I no believe it when your father tell me, so I come see for myself. You bring cookies to wake? Shaped like coffins? Is waste of time. I need fortune cookie. You give me one to open when I get home."

"We'll have to get you some from the private room. But why not open it here?" I asked.

"What, you think I *pazza* too? Open fortune cookie in funeral home, might as well get in coffin. Just like Eddie. Zach tell me all about what happen to him." Nicoletta clucked her tongue like a chicken. "That one—he never very smart. Is no surprise."

"Good grief, Nicoletta," Josie gasped. "The man is dead. Show a little respect."

"Do you know Zach—err, Mr. Stevens well?" I asked.

She nodded. "He good friend of Ronald's. They go fishing together. But they never catch anything. They too old."

Ronald Feathers was Nicoletta's eighty-something-year-old boyfriend. The man had lost most of his teeth and was hard of hearing, but that wasn't necessarily a bad thing where Nicoletta was concerned.

"Do you think you could get Zach to come over here and talk to us?" Josie asked suddenly.

I nudged my friend again. Nicoletta was nobody's fool, and I didn't want to put her on alert.

Sure enough, the elderly woman latched on to Josie's words. "Why you want to see him?" she demanded. Her leathery face watched me closely, even though Josie had asked the question.

"We thought he might want a fortune cookie," I said brightly. "Josie will get him one."

Her expression told me that I wasn't fooling her. "Ha! I knew it. You here to find out who kill Eddie. Same as everybody else."

I cocked an eyebrow. "That's not true. They're here for Mrs. Peacock."

"Baloney," she spat out. "You think people come for that old woman? She nastier than a skunk. Meaner than me."

"That is pretty bad," Josie agreed.

Mrs. Gavelli ignored her. "Everybody want to know who kill Eddie. Your papa tell you to come here. He always with Eddie. Crazies stay with crazies."

"You would know," Josie whispered as Nicoletta made her way over to Zach.

We watched as Nicoletta said something to the man. He looked over at us and then closed the door, practically in a mourner's face. I studied him as he approached. Zach wasn't much taller than me and thin to the point of being gaunt, his face lined with wrinkles. Even at his advanced age, he still had an abundance of snow-colored hair and crystal clear blue eyes that regarded us warmly.

"Well, if it isn't the cookie ladies," he said.

Before we could reply, Mrs. Gavelli pushed herself between us and Zach. "No let the cookies fool you. They here to find out who kill Eddie."

Thanks for the help, Mrs. G.

To my surprise, Zach didn't move away. "You're Dom's daughter, aren't you? The baker, not attorney, right?"

I extended my hand. "Yes. I'm Sally Donovan, and this is my best friend, Josie Sullivan."

"Yah, she own bakery," Mrs. Gavelli cut in. "Her sister the attorney and my granddaughter-in-law. She a whack job too. It run in their family."

I gritted my teeth together to keep a flippant response from tumbling out. As a public defender, Gianna's job was much more stressful than mine. Her son, Alex, had just started walking, and she was having a tough time keeping up with him. On top of that, she had to contend with Mrs. Gavelli most days. She certainly had her work cut out for her.

"It's all right," Zach assured us. "Linda already told me that you'd be here tonight looking into Eddie's death."

Josie and I stared at each other dumbfounded. I thought Linda had understood it was imperative to keep our real reason for being here a secret. So why was she telling her employees, especially when they were under a cloud of suspicion?

"As you're aware, my father was a good friend of Eddie's," I explained. "But we're primarily here to represent our bakery's goods. Dad just thought we might be able to find out some more details of Eddie's death. He's so upset about it."

"We're not detectives," Josie put in.

Zach scratched his head thoughtfully. "I wish I could help, ladies, but there's nothing I can tell you."

"How long have you worked here?" Josie asked.

"About three years," Zach said. "I was employed at Shakey's Funeral Parlor until they went under." He gave us a sly wink. "Sorry, just a little funeral home humor."

"That no funny," Mrs. Gavelli declared.

I nudged Josie again. "Hey, Jos, why don't you take Mrs. Gavelli into the reception so that she can pick out her own fortune cookie?"

Josie immediately got the message. She grabbed the elderly woman's arm and gave me a look that said I'd owe her big-time for this.

Zach waited until they had walked away. "Eddie was a good guy, and I'm going to miss him," he said sadly. "Feel free to ask me anything you like."

"Did Eddie have any enemies that you knew about?"

The elderly man seemed perplexed. "Enemies? Eddie?"

"Okay, maybe that's too strong of a word," I admitted.

"Was there someone who didn't like him very much? A former customer perhaps?"

Zach considered my question for a minute. "Well, there was that whole mess with his brother, Arthur. I mean, he was ticked off about their father leaving the funeral home to Eddie, but I thought he'd moved on. I mean, how long can a person hold a grudge for?"

"You'd be surprised."

He frowned. "Last week, I came into work one morning to find Arthur sitting in Eddie's office, behind his desk, waiting for him."

This was unexpected. "Did Linda know he was here?"

"I'm not sure anyone did," Zach said. "I was the first to arrive that morning—well, after Arthur, of course. Eddie must never have changed the locks. After his brother left, Eddie asked me not to tell anyone he'd been here."

I raised an eyebrow. "Do you know what they were talking about?"

He shrugged. "Not really. When Eddie came in, he shut the door to his office, but I could hear them talking in low voices. Arthur was only here for a couple of minutes. After he was gone, Eddie said something weird to me, like, 'I'm paying for my mistake.'" Zach stared at me in confusion. "What do you think he meant by that?"

The words made me shiver inwardly. Had Eddie known someone was out to kill him? "No idea. I guess there could be several different meanings. Maybe Arthur threatened him? Or he decided to sell the place to him?"

Zach shook his head vehemently. "Eddie would never sell this place. He always joked that he was just like the funeral home's motto—with it to the very end."

"What about the woman who does the makeup— Charlene? Is there any way I can speak to her?"

"Charlene's not here tonight. She usually works during the day. She got Mrs. Peacock in tip-top shape earlier. She's good at her job. Didn't even ruffle one feather on the woman. Ha-ha, get it?"

I struggled not to roll my eyes.

People were crowding the area by the front door, and

some had started rapping on it, but Zach didn't seem to be concerned. Instead, he crooked his shriveled pinky finger for me to come closer, which I reluctantly did. "Want to know a secret?"

No. "Yes."

"Charlene had the hots for Eddie," Zach chortled.

I hadn't been expecting this. "How old is Charlene?"

"Mid-forties. A regular spring chicken." A small smile played at the corners of Zach's cracked lips. "Yeah, she was looking to jump his bones. Isn't that what you young people say?"

"I'm not familiar with the phrase," I muttered.

Zach sighed. "Too bad that's all that's left of him now."

Oh. My. God. I stared at him mutely, too shocked for words.

"She was always trying to get him into her work room," Zach continued. "If you ask me, Eddie should have taken Charlene up on it. She's younger than Linda and way better looking than that old prune."

Zach was the last person who should be calling anyone old, but I refrained from saying so. "When will Charlene be in again so that I can talk to her?"

"About eight o'clock tomorrow morning," he replied. "We've got another wake scheduled for tomorrow night, and her services will be needed. You can watch her do her thing, so to speak. She likes to have company while doing makeovers."

"Sounds good." Who was I kidding? A casual conversation with Charlene while she puts makeup on a dead person. Yes, that was something I definitely wanted to do first thing in the morning. "What about Wally? Did you get along with him?"

Zach started to laugh. He threw his head back so far that I was afraid he might go into traction. "Wally? Mr. Employee of the Year? He stole from Eddie and then had the nerve to complain about how badly life treated him. What a piece of work."

"Sounds like you didn't like him very much."

Zach's wrinkles deepened. "That's right. I couldn't stand him. Before he came along, I was the hearse driver. That was *my* job until Eddie took it away from me and gave it to that jerk. I told Eddie I didn't want to be a doorman, but he said I was getting too old to drive." His nostrils flared. "Do you know how that made me feel?"

"I'm sure it was nothing personal," I said gently.

Zach drew a handkerchief out of his breast pocket and dabbed at his forehead with it. "I could never understand why Eddie hired him. Why, that guy would sell his own mother for a buck. It was all he cared about. Eddie was usually a smart guy, but Wally managed to dupe him. Too bad he couldn't see that guy for what he was until it was too late. A low-down, dirty skinflint."

I decided to change the subject. "Did you know that the funeral home was having trouble financially?"

Zach's eyes widened in amazement. "What do you mean? The place is doing well. I mean, we have a wake scheduled almost every day this week. That's how we make the cold hard cash, you know."

"True," I agreed, "but I heard that there were money problems. You weren't aware of any?"

"No, ma'am." He gave me an accusing look, as if I was lying. "Eddie was a good businessman. I don't believe that for a second. Now, if you'll excuse me, I have a door to attend to."

I watched Zach fight his way through the crowd and even force a few people back onto the porch with an umbrella from the umbrella stand. For an elderly man, he still had a great amount of stamina. Was he lying when he said he didn't know about the financial problems? It was possible that Eddie had never told him. Zach resented Eddie giving his job to someone else, but was that enough reason to kill him? Or did he have another reason he hadn't divulged?

Josie was approaching with Gianna. I had no idea where she'd come from. My sister wasn't smiling and came right to the point. "This was Dad's idea, wasn't it?"

"How did you guess?" I gave a wry smile.

Gianna shook her head in disgust, her chestnut-colored hair whipping back and forth with the movement. My baby sister was my pride and joy. She was beautiful and intelligent, a successful lawyer and a wonderful mother, but I knew she wrestled with self-doubt on a regular basis.

She lowered her voice. "Sal, this is crazy. Dad has you looking into Eddie's murder, doesn't he?"

"I couldn't tell him no, Gi. It means so much to him."

"But he's being selfish," she protested. "You have a business to run and a baby who isn't sleeping through the night yet."

"It's only for one evening." I tried to make light of the situation. "Cookie has to sleep at some point, right?"

Gianna sighed. "Well, I'm still waiting for Alex to sleep through the night, and he was a year old last month."

She wasn't cheering me up any. "I'm only asking a few questions. Linda said the place was having financial problems, but I'm hearing conflicted reports. Zach, the doorman, acted like he didn't know anything about it."

Josie glanced over at the line of people waiting to sign the guest book on the podium by the front door. "What's a funeral going for these days, anyway?"

"It depends," Gianna said. "Ronald Feathers told Nicoletta that he's already pre-booked his here. It's costing him about ten grand. But I do believe he's asked for the best they have. Bronze casket and organ music with a full Catholic service. Oh, and the reception gig. The works."

I wrinkled my brow. "That's the works?"

"What about Nicoletta?" Josie asked with interest.

Gianna narrowed her eyes. "She's already told Johnny and me that she's never going to die."

"They say only the good die young," Josie said thoughtfully. "She might outlive all of us."

Gianna threw up her hands in pantomime. "That woman is driving me nuts. She called and asked if I could bring her home. Apparently, Ronald dropped her off for the service but couldn't stay because of some poker game, and she's fit to be tied. But does she call him up to come back and get her? Nope. Gianna's on her way home, so she can do it. No problem, right?"

My poor sister. If Nicoletta was in my family, I'd be tempted to throw myself from the nearest bridge. "Where is she now?"

Gianna exhaled sharply. "Talking to Mr. Peacock. They're both griping about the cost of funerals. I wish I'd asked

Grandma to come and get her, but she shouldn't be driving at night. Plus, she's helping Mom with Cookie."

"Sorry about that," I murmured.

She waved a hand in dismissal. "Don't be. Is Dad here?"

"He was earlier," I explained. "He's got blogging to catch up on but told me he expects a full report later tonight."

"Good. It's better if he doesn't hear this yet." Gianna hesitated for a moment. "When Dad told me about Eddie, I decided to do a little digging myself. Sorry about the pun. Anyhow, I didn't like what I found."

"Oh boy," Josie muttered.

"What I'm about to tell you is extremely sensitive," Gianna went on. "I'm not comfortable revealing that information, but my friend Ben Chilson, partner at Chilson & Quincy Law Firm, is getting in touch with the police as I speak."

"Don't keep us in suspense," I urged. "What's going on?"

"I figured Brian would tell you anyway." She frowned as she said his name, and I knew why. Despite his new marital status, Gianna thought Brian was still hung up on me. It was a ridiculous notion. "A local family was in to see Ben last week. They're considering filing a lawsuit against Phibbins Mortuary for theft."

"Theft of what? Dead bodies?" Josie asked excitedly.

Gianna shook her head. "They believe Phibbins Mortuary stole jewelry that belonged to a family member. More specifically, that they snatched jewelry off a loved one's *dead* body."

CHAPTER SEVEN

———

"Eddie was a *thief?*" Somehow, I couldn't picture it, and didn't want to. Never mind what the truth would do to my father. Dad was old-school Italian, and the one thing he couldn't stomach was dishonesty. A few years back, he'd briefly worked as a hearse driver for Phibbins Mortuary, but Eddie let him go when Dad wouldn't stop talking to the mourners. My father had respected Eddie's decision and taken it in stride. He had great admiration for the man, so if this was true, his feelings would undoubtedly change forever.

Josie grimaced. "I've heard about stuff like that happening before. But wouldn't the deceased's loved ones know if an item, say a necklace, was missing before the person is cremated or buried? Do they just assume the jewelry goes with them?"

Gianna's high cheekbones became tinged with pink. "In some instances, yes, people want the jewelry buried with their loved ones. But with the increased chance of looting these days, many want the valuables returned. This particular family asked for the jewelry to be returned but then discovered it was an imitation. You'd be surprised how many people try to get away with something similar, and often it isn't found out until the owner goes for an appraisal or tries to sell the valuables themselves."

"Are there any more families involved? Could they have been so angry with Eddie that they decided to kill him?" Josie asked.

Gianna gave a small toss of her head. "I'm not directly involved and really can't tell you if there are other cases pending. Not until the suit or suits become public knowledge, of course.

In this particular situation, the deceased had their wake and funeral with Phibbins Mortuary about three months ago. The woman's husband claimed that his wife owned a valuable diamond wedding ring worth about ten thousand dollars. The husband needed the money after she died to pay expenses, so he went to have it appraised. The jeweler told him the ring was worthless and its stone was cubic zirconia, so it obviously was replaced at some point."

"Does he have proof that the ring was valuable in the first place?" I hated to think the worst of Eddie.

"That's where this gets tricky," Gianna replied. "The husband didn't give her the ring. It belonged to his wife's grandmother. He's been trying to locate pictures of his wife wearing it, but many of their photos were lost in a recent basement flood. Several other family members are backing up his claim, though. Ben told him to ask relatives for photos before he goes through with the lawsuit."

Josie shook her head in disgust. "Poor guy. It's basically his word against Phibbins Mortuary's."

"Does Linda know?" I asked.

"I'm not sure," Gianna said. "The deceased's husband may have reached out to her. And yes, it's their word against Linda's right now, but if pictures are located and more people come forward, things are going to get ugly pretty fast."

Another headache Phibbins Mortuary didn't need right now. "If the funeral home was having financial problems, I guess Eddie could have done this. But I don't believe it. Heck, I don't want to believe it. Dad said that Eddie always prided himself on honesty."

"I'll let Dad know," Gianna said. "You have enough to deal with already, since he's got you checking into his death. In all fairness to Eddie, though, it may not have been him after all. We can't say for sure."

"Dead men tell no tales," Josie quipped.

That was for sure. "Eddie prepped the bodies for burial, but Linda told us yesterday that all the employees knew how to embalm, even Zach."

"Yikes." Josie frowned. "I wouldn't want that old guy working on me. He'd probably misplace my head."

"Never mind," I said. "Gianna's right. It could have been anyone who had access to the body. Linda, Eddie, Charlene Jones, who does the makeup—"

Gianna's eyebrows shot up. "Did you say Charlene Jones?"

"Yes, she's the cosmetologist here. Do you know her?"

"I represented a Chantal Jones in court last month. She mentioned that she had a twin sister named Charlene, but I've never met her. It's a common surname, so there's always a chance it isn't her."

I was intrigued. "Gi, I know that there's such a thing as attorney-client privilege and understand if you can't tell us what Chantal did, but is there any chance it had to do with stealing?"

"Are you thinking it runs in the family by chance?" Gianna asked as her phone beeped. She drew it out, typed a quick response, and then put it back in her purse. "Thank goodness Johnny's school is on break this week. I'm late getting home, thanks to having to stop and pick up Nicoletta."

"You get all the good jobs," Josie said dryly.

"You didn't answer my question," I said. "Can you give me a hint as to what Chantal did?"

Gianna's chocolate-colored eyes regarded me solemnly. "It's no secret. There was an article in the paper about her when it happened. Chantal is, *or was*, a server at Jerry's Juice Bar. She was accused of taking other employees' tips, prior to being fired and arrested."

"Wait a second," I interrupted. "Isn't that a topless bar?"

"Yes," Gianna said. "I got her off, but to be honest, I wasn't quite convinced myself that Chantal didn't do it. I don't like representing clients I don't believe in, but a fellow colleague, who is a relative of Chantal's, asked me to take the case since they couldn't. Personally, I'm not convinced that stealing runs in a family, but she and Charlene could have been in cahoots together."

I thought back to the conversation I'd had with Zach earlier. "If Chantal is Charlene's twin—well, something doesn't add up here. Charlene is in her midforties, and she's working in a juice bar? Topless?"

"Some women still have it going on at that age," Josie

remarked. "Look at your mother. She could work in one of those places and make a fortune."

My sister and I both groaned simultaneously. "Please," Gianna said. "Mom likes to parade around in her skivvies, but even she'd draw the line at nudity. She and Dad are strange, but they happen to have morals."

Josie barked out a laugh. "I didn't mean Maria *would* do it, only that there's women older than Chantal who have great figures. Sal and I have some experience in the strip club department, remember."

"Bite your tongue." I didn't want to be reminded of the time Josie and I had chased a possible murderer into a topless club and he'd taken a shine to me. I'd been forced to entertain him while we waited for the police to arrive. It hadn't taken him long to discover that I had no dancing skills to speak of.

Josie's remark about my mother's great figure left me feeling a bit self-conscious, but that wasn't unusual. Josie was never tempted by the array of sweets she baked daily. She said being around them so much killed her appetite. It was just the opposite for me. Gianna herself had gained sixty pounds before Alex's birth but lost it all within three months afterwards.

I sighed and stared down at the black slacks I'd squeezed myself into for the wake. They'd fit fine before the baby but were now so snug that I had to undo the top button. I still had fifteen pounds of baby fat—or Cookie fat—to lose, and my little bundle of joy was already four months old. How did everyone else make it look so easy?

"Charlene's not here tonight, so that means I'll have to make a trip back tomorrow to talk to her," I said.

Gianna's expression was grim. "I knew this wouldn't be a one-time thing. You're in it for the long haul."

I shook my head. "No way. I'm sorry about what happened, but I don't have time to keep looking into Eddie's death. Dad just doesn't understand. The police can handle it without me. Besides, I promised Mike I'd stop all of this when Cookie was born."

"You can't stop. It's in your blood," Josie said. "Like baking is in mine. Like evil is in Mrs. Gavelli's. Like law is in Gianna's—"

"Okay, I get it," I interrupted sharply. "The fact remains that I'm somehow managing to dig myself in deeper."

"Six feet under," Josie laughed. "Sorry, Sal, I couldn't resist."

Gianna nodded in the direction of the viewing room. "Isn't that Eddie's wife headed our way?"

"About time," Josie grumbled. "She's kept us waiting long enough. Yeah, Linda's easy to pick out of a crowd. Can't you see those dollar signs shining in her eyes?"

Linda was wearing an emerald-colored dress with black flowers that hung off her bony frame and looked about two sizes too large. She gave a small wave when she saw us.

"Girls," she squealed. "People are already raving about the desserts! This is going to be such a boost to our cash flow. I'm going to make up a new funeral home package that includes coffin, music, service, and special treats by Sally's Samples. You'll have to come back again tomorrow night."

Not likely.

Gianna took this as an opportunity to make her departure. "Please excuse me. Time to find my psycho grandmother-in-law, Nicoletta, before she makes a scene."

"Too late," Linda said. "Nicoletta's in the viewing room telling anyone who will listen that even hell won't take Mrs. Peacock. The sad part is that Mr. Peacock is agreeing with her."

My sister's face went pale. "Gotta go." She blew me a kiss and rushed into the viewing room.

I turned my attention to Linda, who was straightening the window blind behind us. "Can we talk for a minute?"

"Oh, I'm sorry to have kept you waiting. I'll get you a check right away."

"There's something else." I glanced around, but fortunately we were alone and not attracting a lot of attention, though Zach was eyeing us sharply from his station by the front door. "I've heard a rumor that there's a family considering filing suit against the funeral home for theft."

Linda's smile faded. "What family? That's ridiculous! Where did you hear such a thing?"

"I can't reveal my sources." Even if the police had already been informed, I didn't want to take a chance on getting

Gianna involved.

"You had no idea?" Josie asked.

Linda shook her head. "None. I don't understand. What did they claim was stolen? I mean, there was the issue with Wally stealing urns, but Eddie knew all about that and had him arrested."

"A family of a deceased woman is claiming that Phibbins Mortuary replaced an authentic diamond ring of hers with a fake one," I said.

She frowned. "Impossible. Eddie would never do something like that."

A flicker of discomfort in her amber-colored eyes made me believe that *yes*, Eddie would have done something like that, or else Linda knew who had.

"If you want me to help, you have to trust me," I said.

Linda's jaw went slack, and she lowered her gaze to the floor. "You have to promise that you won't tell anyone."

"It depends on what you're going to say." I had to be honest with her. "Eddie may have been killed over this incident. If you have anything to share, please tell us now because it may help to find his killer."

Josie nudged me in the ribs. "Don't forget the fact that she's been going around telling people why you're here, Sal—namely that old codger, Zach."

Linda thrust her shoulders back in defiance and glared at Josie. "Zach can be trusted. He's worked here for three years—the longest of any employee."

She clearly wasn't getting the message. "The point is there's someone who *can't* be trusted. You can't keep going around and telling everyone the real reason I'm here if you want me to find out anything."

Unshed tears glistened in Linda's eyes. "I'm sorry," she wailed. "I thought that Zach might be able to help. He was upset about being demoted, but he adored Eddie and—" Her shoulders sagged as if she had the weight of the world upon them.

A few people leaving the viewing room were watching us curiously. When I patted Linda on the shoulder, she only sobbed harder. "Is there some place we can talk privately?"

She nodded and wiped her eyes. "Of course. Eddie's

office. I need to get your check from there anyway."

Josie gestured for me to go ahead. "I'll see if more coffee is needed. Hopefully, we can clear out soon."

My sentiments exactly. I placed a hand on the small of Linda's back and guided her toward the office, at the rear of the building. The cuckoo clock mounted on the wall sang out eight times as we passed. *Great.* Mike was going to be ticked. I couldn't blame him, and frankly, I was upset too.

We passed the viewing room on our way, and I stole a quick glance inside. Despite the crowd, I easily picked out Nicoletta standing near the casket talking with Mr. Peacock. My sister was trying unsuccessfully to pull her away. I had an eerie feeling that I was being watched and turned my head. Zach was staring after us. His eyes met mine, and he looked away. I didn't care what Linda said, and Zach's age didn't matter. In my mind, no one at Phibbins Mortuary could be trusted.

Eddie's office was a large room with dark paneled walls, an L-shaped mahogany desk, built-in bookcases, and an oak coffin taking up one entire wall. The lid was open, and someone had placed a pile of magazines on the headrest.

Linda followed my gaze. "It's a display casket," she explained, as if reading my mind. "Did you know that caskets and not coffins are used in viewings?"

"My father keeps a coffin in his house," I said.

She frowned and drew her eyebrows together, as if trying to make sense of this. "Eddie told me your father was a unique individual. But it makes sense he would use a coffin and not a casket. Coffins are smaller than caskets. They're made narrower at the bottom to save money on wood and are usually cheaper for that reason. Caskets look much nicer for an actual service."

"I never knew this."

Linda shrugged as she stood with her back to the desk and gestured for me to sit in the plush velvet chair in front of her. "Neither did I until Eddie told me." She let out a long, ragged breath. "That man knew everything about the funeral business."

"Tell me about the thefts." I hoped I didn't sound as impatient as I felt.

"They can't prove anything," Linda said defensively.

"Eddie might have mentioned a possible lawsuit in passing. Their attorney wrote him a letter, but he didn't think the family would actually go through with it."

"So Eddie did replace the diamond in the ring with a false one?"

Linda twisted a tissue between her hands and wouldn't meet my gaze. It seemed I had my answer. "Linda?"

She still didn't reply. I reached deep down inside myself for some patience but came up empty. I reminded myself that the woman was grieving. "Please be honest. You can trust me. I'm not the police."

Her lower lip trembled. "It's possible, I guess. Eddie had a gambling problem. He owed money to people."

"What people? Bookies?"

A tear rolled down Linda's left cheek as she nodded. "He liked the casinos—a bit too much. No one knew except me. He kept it private and was afraid it might hurt the business. That's why he always went to ones in Niagara Falls and never around here. He was afraid someone might recognize him. Silly, huh?"

I stared at her in disbelief. My father had told me Linda wasn't the sharpest crayon in the box, and that was an understatement. "No, it definitely wouldn't look good, especially if he's being accused of theft. Customers wouldn't trust him and might think he'd cheated them by raising his prices to try to cover his personal debt. You need to tell the police."

She started to sob, and guilt overwhelmed me. "Please don't cry anymore, Linda. What's done is done. How much money did he owe the bookies?"

Linda blew her nose into the tissue. "He wouldn't tell me. Eddie kept me in the dark about a lot of things."

That probably hadn't been too difficult. "So, there may be more families filing suits against the funeral home?"

"It's…possible," she conceded. "I don't know what happened to him this past year. He became so secretive and resentful practically overnight. He wasn't like this at all when we got married. Last month, I threatened to leave him unless he got his act together."

I was startled by her admission. "My father never mentioned that Eddie had an addiction, and he spoke to him almost every day."

"That's because Eddie didn't want him to know," Linda explained. "He looked up to your father. He said Domenic was such a talented man."

Okay, I wasn't going there. "Do you happen to know the names of the bookies that Eddie borrowed money from?"

She shook her head. "He wouldn't tell me. But now that Eddie's dead, I won't have to worry about that anymore, right?"

This gullible woman needed to get her head out of the clouds. I'd once been involved in a murder case where the victim had been found dead in my former bakery. He'd owed money to a mob family who couldn't have cared less about his death. They wanted the cash and would do anything to get it.

"There's more." Linda sniffed. "I think that Eddie was having an—"

"Well, well. Hope I'm not interrupting anything."

Startled, we both looked up. An attractive older man was standing in the doorway, watching us. He was wearing a black designer suit and leather loafers polished so brightly that they shone. His piercing metallic blue eyes came to rest on me.

Linda gasped and pointed at him, her hand visibly shaking. "What are you doing here?"

"I heard voices, so I wanted to see who was in here." The man brushed a hand across his silver-colored hair. "I mean, this should have been *my* business, remember? I've got the right to look around if I want."

A vein bulged in Linda's neck. "This was, and still is, Eddie's office. Now get out of here, and don't ever come back."

It didn't take much effort to figure out who this man was. I rose to my feet and stood in front of Linda, blocking her from the man. "You're Arthur Phibbins?"

He looked me up and down, and his mouth curved into an evil-looking smirk. "That's right. Who might you be, dollface?"

"My name is Sally Donovan. My father is—*was*—a good friend of your brother's."

"Sally," Linda said in a tight voice. "You don't have to explain anything to this man. He's the one responsible for Eddie's death."

CHAPTER EIGHT

————

"You're crazy." The cocky smile disappeared from Arthur's face as he glared back at us. "That's not a nice way to treat your favorite brother-in-law, Linda."

Linda's nostrils flared. "You're my *only* brother-in-law, and you've never been a favorite. I wish to God we weren't related. Now he's dead because of you."

"I didn't kill him," he seethed. "I couldn't do something like that to my own brother, even if we didn't get along. For all I know, it could have been you who killed him. Or one of your idiotic employees."

"You're horrible," she breathed. "All you did was make his life a living hell. I'm betting you came here that day to badger Eddie into selling you the funeral home. You couldn't let up, ever since your father died. Eddie told you to never come back—you got angry and killed him."

Arthur took another step toward us. "Lucky for you I'm not easily offended. Yeah, I wanted the business, but I'd never stoop that low."

"Why are you really here, Mr. Phibbins?" I asked.

His gaze returned to my five-foot-three-inch frame. He looked at me like I was an insignificant piece of lint on his well-pressed suit. "If you must know, I'm actually here to pay my respects to the Peacock family."

"Liar," Linda said angrily. "You're here to make trouble. You need to leave."

"You don't have a choice, Linda," Arthur said smugly. "It's all over town that the mortuary hasn't been doing well. Sell it to me and make yourself a nice profit."

She gave him a look of disgust. "I can't believe your

nerve. Your brother is barely cold, and already you're talking about taking his business over."

Arthur examined her face carefully. "Why are you acting so surprised? It's no secret I've wanted the place for a long time. Plus, you hate the business. Get out while you can."

There was a long pause before Linda spoke again. "Things will get better," she said nervously. "I have Sally helping me. She'll find out who killed Eddie."

Head smack. Why did Linda keep doing this? Was she really that dense?

Arthur gave a low chuckle. "Nancy Drew in disguise? Where's your convertible and blonde hair, honey?"

Before I could retort, Linda prattled on. "Sally owns Sally's Samples bakery. She's solved several murder cases that have managed to elude the police. It's only a matter of time before we get your sorry butt thrown into jail."

Arthur roared with laughter. "Yeah, she looks about as sharp as you, Linda. And that's not saying much."

Anger rose from the pit of my stomach. "There's no need to be insulting. And I believe that Linda asked you to leave."

"Come off it, dear sister-in-law," Arthur chuckled. "Sell the place. None of you know what the hell you're doing without Eddie. You're up to your neck in debt."

Linda started to wring her hands. "I could never sell it, Arthur."

There was a sudden indecisiveness to her tone, which made me think that Linda *was* considering a sale. For the life of me, I couldn't figure this woman out.

"Arthur, it wouldn't be right of me to do it," she went on. "Eddie loved this place. He was devoted to it till the very end."

Arthur snickered at her choice of words. "Yeah, and look what that got him."

"Excuse me, Mrs. Phibbins?" Brian stuck his head in the doorway, and I sighed with relief. "Is there a problem in here?"

"Thank goodness, Officer Jenkins." Linda pointed at her brother-in-law. "This is Eddie's brother, Arthur. He was just leaving."

Brian pursed his lips. "Yes, I was hoping to find you, Mr. Phibbins. Can we have a quick talk before you take off?"

"About what?" Arthur asked sharply.

"I have a few questions about your brother. It won't take long." Brian smiled pleasantly at him and then nodded to Linda. "Ladies, if you'll excuse us for a few minutes?"

I knew better than to ask if I could stay. Brian would never permit it. I gave everyone a careless wave. "I need to be going anyway."

Linda was at my heels as I left the office. She handed me a check. "Oh, Sally, I was hoping you'd be able to stay a little longer. I'd like to talk to you and Josie about doing some more goodies for future receptions. As luck would have it, there's another viewing tomorrow night for Mrs. Perry, and her family would like refreshments set up in our private room afterwards. We expect a good crowd since she used to be a librarian."

My cell beeped. "Excuse me for a second." I pulled the phone out of my pants pocket and saw that there was a new text from Mike. *Picked up Cookie at your parents. We're at home waiting for you. When can we expect you? Midnight?*

Oh boy. Sarcasm practically dripped from his message. With a small sigh, I closed my eyes, feeling defeated. "Not tonight, Linda. I'll call you tomorrow."

*   *   *

"We did great, Sal," Josie gloated as she turned onto my street. "We cleared over four hundred bucks, even after the cost of supplies! Mike can't be upset when you tell him that."

Little did she know. I unbuckled my seat belt as Josie pulled into my driveway. One lone lamp shone in the living room window, and I could see the reflection from the nightlight in Cookie's bedroom. "It won't matter. He's going to be furious when I tell him I'm going back tomorrow to talk to Charlene."

"Then don't tell him," Josie said simply. "Dodie's coming in, remember. Once she arrives, you and I will take off to see Charlene. It will take less than an hour, and he never has to know."

"I don't like sneaking around like that," I confessed. "Marriage is supposed to be based on trust."

She laughed. "Put on a sexy nightgown when you get

inside, and he'll stop caring about it. Trust me."

Even though I was usually a private person about such matters, Josie was my dearest friend, and I needed to talk to someone. "That's part of the problem. I never seem to have time for him—if you know what I mean."

Josie's face broke into a sympathetic smile. "All too well. That's natural when you have a baby. After Danny was born, I told Rob I had a headache for two years."

"I'm sure he thought that was funny," I remarked.

"It will pass, don't worry. Go inside and work your magic. Tomorrow is one hour out of the day that he doesn't have to know about. Besides, your father is counting on you, and the coffin cookies are turning into a freaking gold mine for us. You guys need the money, and frankly, so do I." Her smile twisted into a frown. "Rob's company has been making some cutbacks lately. We're worried he might be next."

I gasped. "What? But Rob's been there almost ten years. Isn't it last hired, first fired?"

"Not always," she admitted. "In this case it might be: *you make more money than the rest of the employees, so time for you to go.*" The freckles stood out on Josie's cheeks like they always did when she was worried. "I know you don't need me dumping this on you, especially now, but I wanted to be honest."

"I'm glad you told me." I reached out and hugged her tightly. "I wish life wasn't so complicated some days."

Josie squeezed my shoulders in return. "Me too. Now go on inside and give your man and baby some attention. I'll open tomorrow and then come by to get you after Dodie gets in. What time will your car be ready at the shop?"

"The mechanic said I could pick it up first thing. I'll follow you over to the bakery, and once Dodie's settled, we'll head over to Phibbins."

"Sounds good. Have a good night, hon."

"You too." I waved from the porch as she drove away, sucked in a deep breath, and turned the doorknob, not sure what to expect. Spike was on the other side, wagging his tail in greeting. I stooped to pet him. "Hi, big guy. Did you take care of things while I was gone?"

He trotted into the kitchen where his bed was located,

while I made my way quietly down the hallway. Cookie's door was open a crack, and I peeked inside. She was sleeping on her back in a pink, footed sleeper. She looked like a little doll. I tiptoed over to the crib and peered down at her. I wanted to kiss her but was afraid to wake her.

"Why were you so late?" A sexy voice spoke softly behind me as Mike's arms went around my waist.

"Hi, sweetheart. I'm sorry." I turned to kiss him and inhaled the spicy scent of his cologne. In the dim light, Mike's blue eyes blazed seductively into mine. He was wearing a pair of plaid boxer shorts and nothing else. I put a finger to my lips as he followed me back into our room.

Mike laid down on our bed and yawned. "She went out like a light on the way home. I think your parents wore her out. Just being in their house is exhausting."

I winced at the remark but had to admit he was right. My parents had the same boundless energy as a pair of three-year-olds.

"Come on." Mike winked. "We haven't had any alone time in three weeks."

"You're keeping track?" I laughed and pulled off my shirt.

He patted the spot next to him in bed. "Sure. What else do I have to do? Now, you're all mine for the night. Nothing is going to stop—"

My phone buzzed from my jeans pocket. I drew it out and stared at the screen. My parents' landline. I pressed *Ignore Call* and placed the phone on my nightstand.

"That's my girl." Mike drew me to him and kissed me. "No more interruptions. And that silly nonsense is all over at the funeral home now, right?"

I hesitated for a second too long.

Mike drew back and waited for my response. "Sal, you're not going back there, right?"

"We cleared over four hundred dollars tonight," I pleaded. "Besides, Josie really needs the money. She said that Rob's job is in jeopardy and—"

My phone buzzed again, and Mike swore softly under his breath. "It's your father, isn't it? Turn the damn thing off, please."

"Okay." I shut the phone off and returned it to the nightstand, not wanting to argue.

Mike fell back against his pillow and grunted. "We finally get an hour alone, and your crazy parents are at it again. Let your father go back to the funeral home with cookies. Hell, he gets people to buy that insane book of his, so why can't—"

The house phone rang, and we both cringed. I jumped out of bed and ran down the hall to the kitchen, afraid the sound would wake Cookie. The caller ID confirmed it was my parents' landline.

"Dad," I hissed into the phone. "Cookie's sleeping. I'll call you back in the morning with a report."

"Sorry, baby girl," he said. "But I just got the weirdest call from Arthur Phibbins. He wants me to meet him for breakfast tomorrow."

What the heck? The guy was rude and condescending to Linda and me, and now he wants to break bread with my father?

Mike leaned against the wall and gestured for me to hang up the phone. "Dad, I promise I'll call you in the morning."

As usual, my father went on as if he hadn't heard me. "Linda called a little while ago. She said Zach told her you were going to talk to Charlene. How about I tag along?"

Boy, news traveled fast. "No, thanks. Josie will be with me when I talk to her. It won't take long."

Mike tapped me on the shoulder. "Who are you going to talk to?"

Oh crap. "Dad, I'll speak to you in the morning. And please don't call the house phone again. Bye." I hung up and turned to face my husband.

Mike folded his arms across his broad chest. "Who are you going to meet with and why?"

"We're just going to have a quick talk with the cosmetologist tomorrow," I explained. "It will be during the day."

A vein bulged in his forehead. "I don't like this Sal. You're getting too involved in this guy's death. It's dangerous, and you have other priorities."

I remembered what Josie had said in the car and reached

up to kiss him. I was so exhausted I could barely keep my eyes open but didn't want to go to bed with him upset at me. Perhaps a little romance would lighten his mood. "Josie will be with me. There's no need to worry." I ran my hands down his bare chest. "Now where were we before my father called?"

Mike backed me up against the wall and kissed me. "Okay, you win. Let's forget about your crazy parents and that weird funeral parlor. It's just you and me tonight, princess."

He swung me up in his arms like he used to before I was pregnant and stumbled for a second. All the cheesecake I'd been eating lately wasn't helping my plight. Mike's breathing sounded labored as he made his way through the living room, my arms wrapped around his neck. He took a step forward, and something crunched underneath his feet. The "Farmer in the Dell" song blasted through the room.

Mike swore and fell to his knees, searching for Cookie's toy radio, almost dropping me in the process. I scrambled out of his arms and fell back onto the floor. I was the first to locate the radio and flicked the switch to off. We both sat there in the darkness, daring not to move and waiting to see what happened first—the apocalypse or our daughter's cry.

After a minute of silence, Mike crawled toward me and pushed me gently on my back. "Damn, that was close." He started kissing me again, marking a path down my neck and chest. "Hey, who needs a bed, right?"

"You're awfully spontaneous tonight, Mr. Donovan," I teased as I kissed him back.

A screaming wail rocked the walls. We froze in our tracks, holding our breaths, and waited. Perhaps we thought if we were very still, the cries would subside as if by magic. Instead, they grew louder and more insistent.

"I'll go to her." I scrambled around, searching for my clothes on the floor.

Mike said nothing as he switched on a lamp. He ran a hand through his hair in frustration. "No, I'll get her. There's still a bottle in the fridge."

"She'll go right back to sleep," I said desperately. "It will just take a few minutes and—"

The look of disappointment in my husband's eyes made

me want to cry as loud as Cookie. Our moment had passed, and the spell was broken. We couldn't seem to catch a break these days.

"Never mind, Sal." Mike's voice was deadpan. "I'll take care of her. Go to bed."

CHAPTER NINE

———

"All right, spill it," Josie said. "You've been quiet all morning. What happened last night?"

The bright blue sky radiated warmth through the minivan windows. Spring had finally sprung in Colwestern, and we were ahead of schedule for once. At the end of April, it wasn't unheard of for us to still have snow, but that wouldn't happen today. It was nine o'clock in the morning, and the temperature had already risen to sixty degrees.

After an already busy morning, we were headed to the funeral home. Dodie, our part-time worker, had arrived at eight o'clock and was capable enough to handle things by herself for an hour or so. She was an older woman in her sixties, pleasant enough, and a talented baker like Josie, but she did have her clumsy moments.

I shielded my eyes from the sun. "Nothing. That's the problem. Cookie woke up before we could even get anything started and spoiled the moment. She refused to take a bottle, so Mike brought her into the bedroom for me to nurse, and then he went to sleep without even kissing me good night."

"Aw, Sal. Don't worry. Things will get back to normal again soon," Josie assured me.

"Define normal," I said. "Because I'm not sure what that is anymore. My life feels like an airplane crashing into the side of a mountain. Cookie cries whenever I hold her, my husband feels neglected, and now my father wants me to find out who killed a mortician and stuffed him into one of his own coffins. Sorry, I haven't got a clue what normal is."

"Okay, that is bad, even for you," Josie admitted. "You do always seem to be in the wrong place at the wrong time, but I honestly think you were born with that kind of luck. It's your destiny."

"Thanks for that." I didn't even attempt to hide my sarcasm.

Josie patted my hand. "Try to think positive. You and Mike both want a big family, so you'll have to get together at some point, right?"

I groaned out loud. "I can't handle one child at this rate, let alone three or four like you. How the heck am I ever going to have more? I'll just have to leave them with my grandmother around the clock. She makes everything look so easy."

"You're doing fine. Hey, even your parents had two kids," Josie remarked thoughtfully. "And you and Gianna aren't screwed up, even if they are. See? There's always a bright side to everything."

We pulled into the almost deserted parking lot. The Peacock funeral wasn't scheduled until eleven o'clock, and there were only a couple of cars present. Linda had told me last night that she was expecting a small crowd to attend the service and burial. She knew as well as we did that most of the attendees last night had been there to get the scoop on Eddie's death.

"What happens to Eddie now? Are they going to have a funeral for him?" Josie asked as if reading my mind.

I eased myself out of the car and locked the door. "I believe he's to be cremated, but Linda can't go ahead with the process yet. The police still aren't sure how he died, and because of the embalming, it's making certain tests difficult to conduct. When the time comes, Linda said it will be a private ceremony."

The hearse was parked near the entrance, ready for action, and I spotted two other cars. One was Linda's blue Ford station wagon and the other a gray SUV, which hopefully belonged to Charlene.

"Did you call your father back?" Josie wanted to know.

We walked slowly toward the entrance together. "Yes, first thing this morning. He's planning to meet Arthur at Denny's at ten o'clock. He asked if I wanted to come along, but I said no. I still don't know why Arthur wants to speak to him, unless he thinks that my father has some kind of influence over Linda and will convince her to sell the funeral home."

"If you ask me, Linda's lacking a bit in the brain department," Josie said. "I'm pretty sure my four-year-old is already smarter than her. Your father told you that she never liked the business, so it's not a surprise if she does decide to sell."

"That's true," I admitted.

Josie adjusted the sunglasses on her face. "Do you think Arthur killed his brother?"

"Hard to say. He certainly had a motive. With Eddie out of the way, maybe he thought Linda would agree to sell the place to him. Even though she says that won't happen, I bet she's thinking about it."

"Kind of a crappy thing to do since Eddie would have been dead set against it." Josie covered her mouth. "Oops. Sorry, Sal. The puns are unavoidable sometimes."

"Poor Eddie. His entire life has been reduced to a pun."

The front door of the funeral home was unlocked. For once there was no Zach patrolling the entranceway, and the place appeared empty. As we stepped onto the thick carpeting, loud voices rang out from the direction of Eddie's office, and we stopped to listen.

"You're a lunatic, did you know that?" a shrill female voice screeched. "What possible reason would I have for murdering your husband?"

Linda's soft voice floated through the air. "You know as well as I do. You propositioned him. For all I know, you might have been sleeping with him."

"No, I wasn't," the other woman said angrily. "And I don't appreciate the accusation. Under the circumstances, I think it's best if I find another job as soon as possible."

"I'd say that's an excellent idea." Linda's tone was mocking. "Maybe you should skip town while you're at it. That would be convenient."

"She must be talking to Charlene," I whispered to Josie.

The other woman raged on. "I'm done talking about this. Besides, I have work to do. I've got to pretty up another old hag like you, and God knows how long that will take."

"You are so disrespectful," Linda shot back. "The sooner you get out of here, the better for the both of us."

A door slammed, and the sound of heels clacking in the hallway grew closer until a tall, willowy brunette came into view. She stopped dead in her tracks when she saw us and drew her pencil thin eyebrows together.

"Are you here for the Peacock funeral?" she said in a not overly friendly voice. "It doesn't start for another two hours."

"Charlene Jones?" I asked.

She looked surprised. "That's me. Who wants to know?"

I held out my hand. "I'm Sally Donovan, and this is my friend, Josie Sullivan. We'd like to ask you a few questions if you have a minute."

Charlene scanned me up and down while I did the same of her. Although in her forties, she looked closer to my age. Her oval-shaped gray eyes regarded us suspiciously, while her pert little nose twitched, showing off a diamond piercing that caught the light from above.

Recognition finally dawned on her face. "Oh, that's right. Linda said you were going to be asking me questions about Eddie's murder. You're some kind of investigator she's hired to work the case."

"That woman just doesn't get it, does she?" Josie mumbled under her breath.

"You're wasting your time," Charlene continued. "I didn't kill Eddie. He was a good boss. I liked him very much." She jerked a finger in the direction of Eddie's office. "But I can't work for that woman. Frankly, it wouldn't surprise me if she's the one who—" She paused and perched her dark glasses at the edge of her nose meaningfully. "If you want to chat, you're welcome to come back to my work area. I have nothing to hide."

We followed her down the hallway and into the Employees Only room. She entered and left the door ajar for us to follow.

Josie gulped. "I'm not sure I want to see her working on a dead body. This type of questioning belongs to your father."

I wasn't thrilled about it either, but it didn't look like we had much choice. Josie was no wilting flower, but everyone had an Achilles heel. "It can't be that bad. Come on. Stick with me."

"Like glue." Josie followed me into the well-lit room and gripped me so tightly by the upper arm that I was afraid she might cut off my circulation.

Charlene was standing next to an oak finish casket. I knew it was referred to as a split couch model because my father had explained the differences to me. The head segment of the casket had been left up for viewing purposes, and sure enough, there was a person inside. Josie gave a little squeak as the woman's upper body came into view. "Who—who is—*was* that?"

Charlene turned around, makeup brush in hand, and smiled. "No reason to be upset, hon. She can't hurt you. Meet Cady Perry. Cady, this is Josie and Sally."

"I didn't even know that she'd stopped singing," Josie wondered out loud. "How'd she get so old so fast?"

Charlene gave a loud giggle. "Not *the* Katie Perry. Good Lord, I've never worked on anyone that famous before. I'd be a nervous wreck. No, this Cady was a librarian in Colgate for many years. Her son wanted Phibbins Mortuary to do the service because we have better rates than her town. Hey, it's all about saving a buck, right? Cady died of natural causes. Not like poor Eddie." She sighed and began to touch up Cady's ghost-like cheeks.

I hoped Charlene was in the beginning stages of working on Cady because the woman desperately needed a makeover. There were severe deep wrinkles all over her face, and by the looks of the woman, she must have been near one hundred. Or older, if that was possible.

"She needs sun badly," Josie whispered.

"Yeah, I'll take care of that," Charlene assured her. "The old gal just got her limbs massaged so that rigor mortis doesn't set in. She's been shaved and is all ready for me to make her pretty."

Good grief. I looked away from Cady and stared at Josie's face. She was frozen in place, her eyes transfixed on Cady Perry. It was obvious she wanted to be somewhere else. Anywhere else.

"Thank goodness I'm great at my job," Charlene noted. "Between her and old lady Peacock yesterday, I've really had my work cut out for me this week."

I gulped. "Uh, have you always wanted to work in

funeral cosmetology, Charlene?"

"Yep," she said cheerfully as she styled Cady's coarse white hair. "When I was a little girl, I had one of those Barbie styling heads. Oh my Lord, I loved that thing to death." She flushed. "What I mean is that I did Barbie's makeup every day. She didn't even look like Barbie when I finished with her. One day I even made her up to look like a Ken doll. You could say it's my true calling in life."

My stomach twisted, and for the first time ever, I was sorry that I'd eaten two pieces of Grandma Rosa's cheesecake for breakfast. "How long have you worked here?"

"About two years." Charlene glanced up and laughed when she saw Josie's face. "No offense, honey, but you're pale as a corpse. Sorry—we have to crack jokes in a business like this to keep ourselves sane."

"I think I might be sick," Josie mumbled.

Charlene continued working on Cady. "Eddie was always pleased as punch with my work. Before Phibbins, I was employed at The Eternal Life Funeral Home. Eddie was in there for a viewing and was so impressed with the makeup job on their latest customer that he asked the owner who'd done the work. Greg gave him my name, and Eddie called me. I think Greg regretted telling him about me afterward. Eddie invited me to come and view the funeral home and told me he needed a new cosmetologist. He offered to match what I was making and assured me I'd get occasional raises. Too bad he didn't keep that part of the bargain. I wanted out of Eternal Life, so I accepted the job."

"Any idea who wanted Eddie dead?" I asked.

Charlene's face grew somber. "Eddie was a lovely man. He didn't deserve this. Sure, he may have had people who didn't like him, but doesn't everybody?"

"Did you know his brother at all?" I asked.

"Oh sure." Charlene rubbed some lotion on Cady's forehead. "That guy is a joke. He was always coming around here and harassing Eddie. But I don't think he's a killer."

Josie, who had backed up into the corner of the room closest to the door, suddenly spoke up. "What about the guy stealing the urns?"

"Wally?" Charlene frowned. "Hmm. I guess it's possible. He'd do anything for a buck. I mean, he was using the hearse as a taxicab, for goodness sake. I think Eddie knew, but he was trying to give the guy a break. See, that's the problem. Eddie was too nice for his own good. But when he heard about the urns being stolen, that was the last straw. Then the creep tried to turn things around on Eddie, saying he'd ruined his life!"

"Where we can find Wally?" I had one eye on Charlene and the other on Josie's ghost-like face.

Charlene reached into an open bag of Doritos on the makeup table next to her and shoved a couple into her mouth. *Ew. I* found it unsettling that she was eating while working on a dead person. There must be health codes she was violating. Then again, Cady Perry probably didn't mind, so maybe I should keep my mouth shut.

"His wife left him, you know," Charlene went on. "Wally's a loser, so who can blame her? Yep, dropped him like a hot frying pan when she found out about his little bad habit. Wally's awaiting trial, but it keeps getting pushed back. What's up with that?"

"No idea." Gianna had told me that there were too many court cases and not enough time, but I didn't mention this. I had to think up an excuse to go and talk to the man. Maybe my father could figure into this equation. He'd met Wally before, so he could do the questioning, but Dad would insist on my going along. I sighed. There was no winning for me. "Where did you say he lived?"

Charlene crunched on a chip. "On Stuffle Street. A little blue ranch house. Cute place. His wife took off and stuck him with the bills." A broad grin spread across her face. "Good for her. That's how you can tell someone really hates their spouse—when they're willing to part with a house."

I chose my next words carefully. "I heard that there might have been some other incidents of stealing going on here. Do you know anything about that?"

Charlene looked up with a start, her eyes boring into mine. My face warmed at the contact, so I averted my eyes to Cady Perry. The woman was no rock star, but she looked a heck of a lot better now than when we'd come in. "You do great work."

"Thanks." She spoke quietly, but I noticed that the powder brush shook slightly in her hand. "If anything was stolen around here, you can bet that it was Wally. Or that money-grubbing wife of Eddie's."

I thought about the argument we'd walked in on. "You're not fond of Linda, are you?"

"Hardly." Charlene stared down at Cady, her mouth twisted into an angry frown as if she saw Linda instead. "She didn't deserve Eddie. He cared about his clients, employees, and people in general. He would give you the shirt off his back if you needed it."

Her mouth started to quiver, and Josie and I exchanged glances. Was it possible that Zach had been right, and Charlene was carrying a torch for her boss? Eddie was at least twenty years older than she, but that didn't matter. Charlene had just given a testimony of the qualities she admired about the man.

"Were you having an affair with him?" Josie blurted out suddenly.

I closed my eyes in frustration. Too bad Josie wasn't in nudging range. My friend wasn't known for her tact, but she should have realized this was one of those questions better left unasked.

Charlene's eyes practically bugged out of her head. "What did you say?"

"Ah, she's such a kidder." I started to laugh, and Josie joined in, but she sounded more like a nervous hyena. "I once had a crush on an older man, and Josie still loves to tease me about it."

"His name is Ronald Feathers," Josie put in.

Jeez, she couldn't come up with a fictitious name? Ronald was a friend of Zach's, after all. If this got back to him, I might have to strangle Josie. Even worse, if Mrs. Gavelli found out, she'd be outraged, thinking I was after her man.

Charlene was clearly not amused. Her eyes were dark and brooding at they met mine. "I think it's time that you both left now."

"Josie didn't mean anything by that," I protested. "She just…"

Charlene selected a nail clipper from her makeup tray and turned her back on me. " Good luck finding out who killed Eddie, because you're going to need it."

CHAPTER TEN

––––––

"Charlene simply has to be the one." My father chewed thoughtfully on one of Josie's jelly cookies while absently brushing crumbs off his Sally's Samples sweatshirt. The navy-colored hoodie was a bit snug around his middle since he enjoyed our cookies on a regular basis.

Dad removed another cookie from the bag he'd asked me to bring along and stared out the passenger window of my car. "Yep. It would fit. But I'm not ruling Wally out either. I'm glad you asked me to come along to see him, baby girl."

I gritted my teeth and said nothing. Josie had gone back to the bakery, somewhat relieved to be free from funeral homes and dead bodies for a while. As if he were psychic, my father had phoned to fill me in after his get-together with Arthur. I'd bitten the bullet and asked if he'd like to accompany me to visit Wally. I should have stayed out of this. After all the insinuations from people that my parents were crazy, I might not be far behind.

"This is it, Dad." I stopped for a red light, and my stomach rumbled as the smell from Burger Bob's drifted through my half-opened window. "I can't keep running around asking questions about Eddie's murder. I'm sorry, but there's too much going on in my life right now."

He popped another cookie into his mouth and made a face. "Come on. What am I going to do without you? You're my only hope to solve Eddie's murder. People open up to you, baby girl. When Colwestern residents see a cop coming, they run the other way. Trust me. Everyone's got something to hide."

"Even you?" I couldn't resist.

He chuckled. "Nope. Your author old man is an open

book. Ha-ha. Get it?"

I struggled not to roll my eyes. "Tell me about breakfast with Arthur. What did he want to talk to you about?"

A grin spread across his face. "He wants to advertise on my blog when he buys the funeral home from Linda."

"What?" I asked in disbelief. "Linda hates him. She said she'd never sell to him."

"Arthur seems to think that she will," Dad said thoughtfully. "He believes Linda has no choice in the matter. The place is in the red, and he's got money to make the problems go away. Eddie never told me how bad things were. Jeez, you think you know a person."

"He might have been embarrassed."

His expression sobered. "But I thought things were fine. I still refuse to believe Eddie was stealing from his customers. He was a stand-up guy. It had to be someone else," Dad insisted.

"What did Arthur offer to pay you? Where's he getting the money from? I don't even know what he does for a living."

My father puffed out his chest. "As for what he's paying me, I don't like to discuss financial details, baby girl. Professionals never kiss and tell."

Oh brother.

He went on. "Arthur's retired from a state job. He has interests in a couple of local businesses and has been investing money he received from his wife's life insurance policy. She passed away ten years ago."

"How did she die?" I asked with interest.

"Car accident," Dad said. "And no, he wasn't driving. I know how that suspicious mind of yours works."

"Arthur received nothing when his father died?"

"We talked about that." Dad nodded. "As Linda mentioned, Arthur and his father had a huge argument right before Horace's death. Horace was always on the conservative side. Arthur wanted to try some new things at the mortuary to bring in more business, and the old man was dead set against it. He wants to expand the building, sell mourning clothes, and provide snacks for friends and family."

I still couldn't wrap my head around the idea of selling food at a funeral home. At least my cookies were only being used at receptions. Wasn't it bad enough that Charlene had been eating Doritos while making up a dead woman?

My father broke into my thoughts. "When Horace refused to budge, they got into an argument, and things turned ugly. Arthur said he has a lot of regret now."

"I'm not so sure." I pulled onto Stuffle Street and started looking for Wally's house. "Don't let this guy suck you in, Dad. I don't trust him. He and Eddie didn't get along. Why would you believe him?"

"He doesn't strike me as a killer," Dad said. "I can read people well, Sal. Now, that Charlene I don't trust. She always had that doe-eyed look around Eddie. Plus, she and Linda never got along."

I slowed the car at the side of the road. "You're sure Eddie wouldn't cheat on Linda? I mean, Charlene is attractive, and Linda—" I struggled to find the right words.

He nodded gravely. "Yep. Sort of like a truck ran her over."

"Dad! That's so mean."

He put his palms up in the air. "What can I say? I mean, they all can't be lookers like your mother. I really hit the jackpot with her." He guffawed and patted my knee. "And you and your sister, of course. Three beauties. I'm a lucky man."

We walked up a short gravel driveway that led to the house. The ranch was small but looked well-tended. A metal fence surrounded the lawn to the side and ran around the back of the house. Wicker furniture had already been placed on the wooden porch, and an open bag of mulch sat on the steps. Wally was an optimist. No one even thought of planting flowers around here until June because of the unsettling weather.

We climbed the steps and rang the doorbell. No answer.

"Maybe he's not home," I said.

My father was not about to be deterred. He pushed the bell in with his finger and held it there. After a few seconds, the door was jerked open by a man not much taller than me. For some reason I'd been expecting a strapping six-foot and three-hundred-pound brute of a man.

"Hello, Wally," my father greeted him.

The man's gaze traveled from me to my father and

lingered there. Wally had a handlebar mustache, a head full of thick dark hair, and beady little eyes like a rodent. His voice gave the impression that he'd just smoked a pack of Marlboros. "What do you want, old timer?"

"Do you remember me?" Dad asked.

Wally's bushy eyebrows shot up. "Dom Muccio, right? Yeah, Eddie's buddy. What's this about?"

Dad patted my arm. "This is my daughter, Sally Donovan. She owns Sally's Samples. I'm sure you've heard of the place. It's the bakery that makes the awesome fortune and coffin cookies."

Wally made a face. "Sounds like a nut job bakery if you ask me. It must run in the family. Linda used to say that about you, Dom."

"Hey," my father said. "There's no reason to be insulting."

"What exactly did Linda tell you?" I asked curiously.

He glared at me. "Why should I tell you anything? The entire town knows that I'm awaiting trial. You're not here because you care about me or the hell I've been through."

A thief looking for sympathy. Yes, it certainly took all kinds.

My father held out his hand to shake Wally's. "Come on. Can we come in and talk for a minute? We might be able to help."

I was starting to regret our decision to come here. What did we really know about Wally except that his wife had left him, he'd driven a hearse for Eddie, and hocked his urns on eBay? His biography wasn't scoring any points with me. And he had the nerve to say my bakery was a nut job?

Wally slammed the door into the wall and gave us a mock bow. "Oh please, do enter. But make it fast. I've got things to do."

"I'm sure you have," my father said matter-of-factly and then whispered into my ear. "Especially if he's going to prison soon."

"Dad, stop it," I said.

Wally slammed the door behind us. "All right. You said you could help me. Get to the point."

Although the outside of the house looked adorable, the inside left a few things to be desired. Wally's dining room table was littered with empty beer cans, the entire house smelled of cigarette smoke, and the room was overrun with cobwebs.

Wally sat down at the table and cracked a beer open. "Well?"

"Because of the arrest, you must be aware that the cops suspect you in Eddie's murder," I said.

Wally took a long swig from the can and rocked back in his chair. "Yeah, honey, I already know this. But I didn't kill Eddie. Sure, I was angry at him. He promised me a raise and then never delivered. So I helped myself to one."

Where did he get his nerve? "You stole his property. That's a little different. Rumor has it that you blamed him for your wife leaving."

Wally pondered my statement. "Nah, I didn't really blame him. I was upset, that's all. Old Eddie was cheap but not a bad guy." He blew out a sigh. "I'm going to prison. There's no way around it. Eddie's dying makes it easier for the cops."

"How so?" I asked.

Wally let out an ear-piercing belch. "Everyone knows the police department's overloaded. They're going to try to pin this job on me. Hey, why not? I'll be doing jail time anyway, so why not go ahead and add a longer sentence?"

"It doesn't work that way," I said.

He snorted. "Wake up, honey. This is the real world."

I tried another attempt. "Look, we want to find out who did this to Eddie, so maybe we can help you if you help us in return."

"Yeah? Like how?"

"If you didn't kill him," I said carefully, "who do you think did?"

Wally ran a hand over his greasy-looking mustache. "I'm betting on his brother. See, Arthur had the biggest motive. He was practically foaming at the mouth to get his hands on Phibbins Mortuary. The guy would drop by any time he felt like it, came to every wake, just as an excuse to hang around when he knew Eddie didn't want him there."

"Yes, I've seen that firsthand," I said dryly.

Wally snapped his fingers. "I just remembered something. The day before I got fired, I overheard a conversation between Eddie and Charlene. It sounded like she was propositioning him."

My father poked me in the ribs. "You see? What did I tell you?"

Good grief. "What do you mean, propositioning? Do you think they were having an affair?"

Wally shrugged. "Hard to say. Charlene kept talking in that real sugary voice of hers, saying things like, 'Why don't you come over to my place and let me make dinner—then we can cozy up for the evening.' But Eddie was having none of it. He told her flat out that he was a married man and that, no matter what happened, he would never look at another woman."

My father nodded, a pleased look on his face. "What'd I tell you, baby girl. Eddie was true blue."

"Yeah, a real prince," Wally said bitterly. "Make that a cheap prince. If he'd given me a raise, I wouldn't have had to take it for myself."

I couldn't believe this guy was making excuses for stealing Eddie's property. "Did you overhear anything else between the two of them?"

Wally crushed the empty beer can in his hand. "Not really. Only that Eddie told Charlene he was flattered by the attention but she should look elsewhere. He said she was wasting her time with him. Oh, wait a second. She did say something kind of strange."

"What was it?" my father asked eagerly.

"Charlene told Eddie that he should take a chance. Something about it being sad that he was incapable of living outside the box." Wally stared directly into my eyes. "She said he might be wasting the last precious moments of his life."

CHAPTER ELEVEN

———

"I knew we'd be back." Josie pulled her minivan into the parking lot of the funeral home. "You simply can't tear yourself away, Sal. It's got a hold on you."

"Oh, for goodness sake." My tone sounded defensive. "What was I supposed to do when Linda called and asked me for more cookies? Like you said, it's easy money."

She laughed. "I'm only teasing. You did the right thing. Those coffin babies are a gold mine. Even better than the fortune cookies because these make us actual money." She put a hand to her mouth. "Oops. I bet I've angered the fortune cookie gods now."

I grabbed a tray of cookies out of the back. "We're just going to drop these off and then get the heck out of there."

"Is she writing us a check again?" Josie asked. "Because frankly, after all the talk about Eddie's financial difficulties, I'm starting to get a little nervous. I hope it doesn't bounce."

We made our way toward the front entrance. "I think it's fine. In the future, I'll ask her to pick the cookies up at the bakery. We don't have time to drop these off every night, and Mickey told me he wants to cut back on making deliveries for the next few weeks while he studies for his college exams." Plus, if I spent another evening at Phibbins Mortuary, my husband would not be pleased.

"Hang on a second, Sal. I need to fix my bracelet."

I turned around. Josie was still at the back of the van, fooling with the clasp of the delicate gold rope around her slim wrist. Tiny ruby hearts dangled from it. Rob had given her the piece for Valentine's Day. Josie adored it, even though she rarely wore jewelry.

"It's so pretty," I told her.

"I love that Rob's trying to be thoughtful, but it's unpractical, especially when I'm baking all day. I only put the bracelet on this morning because Rob complained I never wear it. Men. I swear, he gets offended by the littlest things." She jiggled her wrist. "The clasp seems loose. Maybe I should take it to the jeweler."

"We can stop over there after leaving here if you like."

Josie clutched the cookies in one hand and slammed the van door with the other. "No, I'll take care of it tomorrow. Making all the coffin cookies has us behind."

"Don't be silly. We can stop. It will only take a few minutes."

"Forget it. I'm more interested in making money. This is one of those weeks that we need to pull in all the dough we can."

Zach was stationed at the front door, which I found a bit odd since the wake didn't start for another six hours. He really took his job seriously.

"Hi, Zach. How are you?" I greeted him.

He frowned and averted his eyes. "Good day, ladies. Linda is in her office if you need to see her."

His attitude was profoundly different from the other day and I wasn't sure why.

"What's the matter with you?" Josie asked.

Zach snickered but didn't answer.

"Have we done something to offend you?"

He rolled his eyes at me. "If you'll forgive me for saying so, miss, I find your behavior extremely deplorable."

My eyebrows knitted together. "What's deplorable about bringing cookies here?"

Zach gave me a look of disgust. "Forget the cookies. I'm beyond shocked by your actions. My goodness, he's at least forty years older than you. Why, he could be your grandfather. Plus, you're a married woman. Your father is always in here bragging about you and your bakery. I never took you for a tramp."

Josie barked out a laugh. "Sal, do you have a new boyfriend that I don't know about?"

Who was at least forty years older than me? Oh no. Zach must have heard the rumor about Ronald Feathers. His fishing partner, friend, and according to Josie, my main squeeze. I didn't know whether to laugh or cry. "Zach, I'm not carrying on with Mr. Feathers. Josie was only joking around. We're in a hurry, so I'll explain later."

"You young people are always in a hurry." Zach turned up his nose at us. "No common decency these days."

I mumbled an apology and pushed Josie in the direction of the office.

"Hey, take it easy! I don't want to drop these," she exclaimed.

"This is all your fault," I hissed. "Because of that comment you made to Charlene, now everyone here thinks I'm lusting over an eighty-year-old man."

Josie started giggling so hard that I feared she *would* drop the tray. "Come on, Sal. Why would people believe that? Have they seen your husband?"

"It doesn't matter. People in this town love all types of sordid gossip. They thrive on it. And once Mrs. Gavelli finds out—"

"There will be some serious hair pulling and swearing in Italian," Josie teased. "You won't have a chance."

"Yeah well, thanks for that."

We reached the door to the office.

"What did you tell Mike?" Josie asked. "Does he know you're here?"

"I didn't tell him anything. He's meeting me at my parents' house tonight for dinner and thinks we're at the bakery all day. By the way, I'm bringing Cookie to work either tomorrow or the next day. Grandma Rosa has a doctor's appointment, but I'm not sure which day."

She smiled. "It's your bakery, hon, so I guess you can do whatever the heck you like. Maybe we can put Cookie to work."

I raised my free hand to knock. "All in good time."

"Please come in," a voice called.

Linda was sitting in the swivel chair behind Eddie's desk, going through some paperwork. She looked up at us, a broad smile in place. "Hello, girls. How wonderful that you brought the coffin cookies. We've had mourners calling ahead, asking if there would be any after the service tonight."

Jeez Louise. "You mean they're coming for the cookies and not the deceased?" This was a bit disturbing.

She shrugged. "What can I tell you? It happens. So how much do I owe you?" Linda reached into a desk drawer and withdrew a leather checkbook.

I gave her the amount. "Have you heard anything from the police about the cause of Eddie's death?"

"They think it's poisoning, but they don't have all the tests back yet." She stared at me with new interest. "Your father said that he was meeting with Arthur this morning. What was that all about?"

Jeez, couldn't anyone keep a secret? "I'm not sure."

"Right." She obviously didn't believe me. "If I were to wager a guess, Arthur wants to start advertising on your father's blog. He's already making plans for the day he takes over here."

Josie and I exchanged baffled glances. "Is that going to happen?" I asked.

She handed me the check. "Unfortunately, yes. I'm being pushed into a corner. With all of Eddie's gambling debts, the place is in the red. I don't see a way around selling, and Arthur is the only party currently interested in buying it." Linda lifted her eyes to the ceiling. "I hope Eddie will forgive me."

"But you said you'd never sell," Josie pointed out.

Linda's voice was agonized. "What do you want me to do? Do you think it's easy for me? I have to eat, you know."

"No one is judging you," I said gently. "Didn't Eddie have a life insurance policy?"

She shook her head. "He was always too busy with everyone else's death to plan for his own."

Josie raised an eyebrow. "How very morbid of him."

Linda ignored the comment. "I'm taking the money I have left over after paying all the debts—which won't be much—and going to live with my son in England." There was a catch in her voice. "I need to get away. Far away from here."

* * *

"Sweetheart, you've barely touched your dessert." My mother added a coat of bright red lipstick to her mouth as she addressed my father.

Dad pushed his piece of tiramisu away and poured some anisette into his coffee. "I'm not hungry tonight, hot stuff."

We all looked up from our plates in shock. My father saying that he wasn't hungry was like not having snow in Buffalo during the winter. It simply didn't happen.

Mike and I were seated on one side of my parents' cherrywood dining room table, with Cookie on my lap. I had just started her on small portions of baby cereal, as Grandma had advised, and she seemed to be enjoying the taste. How I hoped this helped her sleep better.

Gianna and Johnny were on the other side of the table with Alex, who was busy smearing applesauce on the back of his high chair. Gianna set some Cheerios on his tray, which he immediately shoved into his mouth. My mother and father were both seated at the head of the table while Grandma Rosa's chair at the foot was empty. She'd gone into the kitchen to answer the house's landline.

My mother reached over and laid a hand on my father's arm. He lifted wounded eyes to hers and then pinned me with a stare. "Sal, the police won't share any information about Eddie's murder with me," he complained.

"Dad, you're not related to him," Gianna said.

He sipped his coffee. "How are Sal and I supposed to solve his murder if I don't have any of the facts?"

Mike's fork clattered against his plate. He'd been unusually quiet all evening, and I worried he might erupt like a volcano at any second.

"Look, Domenic," he said sharply. "I don't want Sal involved in this anymore. She has enough going on in her life. Let the police handle it. They'll keep you updated."

My father straightened up in his chair. "Baloney. The cops are being stingy with details. They haven't even given Linda an update."

Gianna sipped her glass of red wine thoughtfully. "It may be that there's no news to share. We assume that someone who worked at Phibbins must have done it. I mean, how many people know how to embalm?"

My mother put her lipstick away in her cosmetic bag and

gave a little shiver. "It's so horrible. Who could do such a thing? Eddie was a lovely man."

I wiped Cookie's face with a burp cloth. She started to fuss, so I rubbed her back until she let out a loud burp, which made everyone laugh.

"A lot of people had motives," I said. "There's Wally, the former driver, who was stealing the urns and then had the nerve to blame Eddie for ruining his life. Zach, the doorman, may have resented him for taking his driving job away. And of course, Arthur wants the family business so bad that he can taste it."

My father nodded vigorously. "That's all true. Don't forget Charlene, who was carrying a torch for Eddie. Or Linda."

Mike looked at him strangely. "What would be Linda's motive? I thought she didn't even want anything to do with the funeral home."

My father pulled the plate of tiramisu back toward him and took a small bite. "Well, it's always the wife, isn't it?"

"You're wrong, dear." My mother smiled at him. "They always say it's the butler."

Grandma Rosa came back into the room and started to clear the table. I gave my squirming daughter to Mike and stood to help her, but she waved me away. "Sit and relax, *cara mia*. You look very tired."

"She is tired," Mike said grimly as he held Cookie on his lap. "She's too busy to keep running over to that funeral parlor. Find another partner, Dom."

"Mike," I whispered. "Please don't start anything."

"She's helping out her old man," my father insisted. "How would you feel if a friend of yours was murdered? It's only natural I'd want the best detective in the state helping me."

"Sal is not a detective," Mike said hotly.

I was afraid World War III might break out. "Dad, I appreciate the vote of confidence, but Mike's right. I'm not a detective. I think it's time to leave this to the police." I sat back down and reached over to take Cookie from Mike, certain that my speech would make him happy, but his face remained stoic. Cookie had quieted in her father's arms, smiling broadly at the lights of the chandelier above, but as soon I lifted her, she started to cry.

Mike held out his arms. "I've got her, Sal."

Having no choice, I handed the baby back to him, and Cookie immediately calmed. What was I doing wrong? Maybe she sensed how frustrated I was with everything. I simply had to do better. I owed my child more. "Dad, if Linda wants more cookies, she can come to my shop from now on. No more deliveries. I'm sorry about Eddie, but I have to put my family and business first."

Mike shifted Cookie to his left arm and drew me toward him with his right one, placing a kiss on the side of my head. "Hallelujah. Princess, you've no idea how happy that makes me to hear that."

My father said nothing. He stared down at his plate with a morose look then pushed it aside and rose from the table.

"Domenic, where are you going?" my mother asked.

"To bed," he announced without turning around. "No one here cares about my feelings."

My grandmother shook the cake server at him. "Stop acting like a baby. If you are so upset about Eddie's death, then you go and find his killer. Leave Sally alone. If she got herself into danger, how would you feel—"

She never finished the sentence. A loud banging commenced on the kitchen door, followed by a woman's scream. We all froze in terror. Grandma Rosa was the first to recover and hurried into the kitchen.

"That's Gram!" Johnny yelled. He left Alex playing with the Cheerios on his tray and rushed out into the kitchen, with Gianna and me following.

My grandmother opened the door to a sobbing Nicoletta, who was wearing a long, black cotton nightgown. Her bare feet stuck out from underneath it, and with shock, I realized this was the first time I'd ever seen her without her Birkenstocks.

Nicoletta clung to my grandmother, crying. "My house. It is on fire!"

Johnny ran toward his grandmother's home. I rushed into my parents' backyard with my sister, and we stared over at Nicoletta's house. The sun had begun to set behind it while smoke was billowing out of her front windows, forming its own dark cloud.

"I'll call 9-1-1!" Gianna ran back inside.

Mike handed Cookie to me and, without a word, sprinted off after Johnny.

"Where are you going?" I screamed. "Let the fire department handle it!"

He didn't answer me. Johnny was already unrolling his grandmother's garden hose from the caddy in her backyard. He shouted something to Mike, and they both tore around the side of Nicoletta's house. My father stood silently beside me, and my mother appeared a second later with Alex in her arms. Cookie started to whimper as Gianna reappeared and took Alex from my mother. "The fire department is on their way."

My grandmother had an arm around Nicoletta's shoulders. After a couple of minutes of sheer terror, the smoke started to disappear. We all breathed a sigh of relief.

"Thank God," Gianna murmured into Alex's hair. "It looks like they got it in time."

"How did it start?" I asked.

The elderly woman wiped at her eyes with a tissue my grandmother had provided. Grandma Rosa was always prepared for disasters. "I upstairs in bed and hear a crash. Then come down and see big hole in my living room window and fire on the floor."

"Who would do such a thing?" my mother wanted to know.

"Crazy kids these days," Dad growled. "Everyone's nuts, I tell you."

My stomach twisted. For some reason, I wasn't convinced that this was a random act by a bunch of kids.

A siren wailed in the distance, and Cookie started to cry as I cuddled her in my arms to no avail. We watched as a fire truck pulled into Nicoletta's driveway. Johnny ran over to meet them and said something to one of the firefighters, who followed him inside the house. I couldn't see Mike, and my anxiety began to increase.

After another minute, we watched a police car pull up next to Nicoletta's mailbox, its red and blue lights flashing, and I cringed inwardly. Of all the worst luck. I knew that car and its number. Brian and his partner, Adam, rushed out of the vehicle and toward the house, but not before I saw Brian's eyes shift in our direction. He shook his head in disbelief and then followed Adam inside.

I kept bouncing Cookie, who had finally started to calm down. Mike ran back over to us. "What happened? Are you okay?" I asked.

He nodded and wiped at the perspiration on his brow with the sleeve of his shirt. "The fire's out. Brian and Adam are inside with the firefighters. Johnny and I were able to put it out with the garden hose. It could have been a lot worse."

"You good boy." Nicoletta nodded at him in approval. "Sally finally do something right in her life."

Grandma Rosa had gone inside and returned with a pair of slippers and a robe from her closet for Nicoletta. The sun had gone down while we were outside, and the temperature was dipping into the forties. "Come," she said. "Some coffee will do us all good."

We all traipsed into the house and gathered around the dining room table. No one spoke as Nicoletta helped herself to a large piece of tiramisu.

I turned to my husband. "What exactly happened?"

Mike gratefully accepted a cup of coffee from Grandma Rosa. "I'm not sure what it was that came through the window," he said, "but the house smells of smoke, and the furniture in the living room is blackened. Brian said he'd be over shortly to fill us in."

As if on cue, the door of the kitchen slammed, and Brian appeared with Johnny behind him. Brian accepted a cup of coffee from my grandmother while Johnny headed right for the wine bottle and helped himself to a glass.

Brian stood next to me and addressed Mike. "That was quick thinking on yours and Johnny's part. If you hadn't gotten to the fire so soon, the whole place could have gone up in flames."

Nicoletta finished her cake and rose from the table. Her leathery-looking face had turned a sickly white, and despite her snarky comment to me, I was filled with pity for her. She stared at Brian hopefully. "I go back home now?"

Brian shook his head. "Not tonight. There's too much damage, and it's not safe. The arson inspector will be out first thing in the morning to file a report. We do know what started the fire, though. Someone threw an M-80 through your window."

"What's that?" my mother asked, puzzled.

"A powerful firecracker," he explained. "It could have burned the house down."

Nicoletta drew a shaky breath. "It those bad kids who live down the street," she declared. "I could have been killed, and no one care."

"You know that is not true," Grandma Rosa scoffed.

My father reached for another piece of tiramisu. It seemed that only certain types of tragedies affected his appetite, and Nicoletta's fire wasn't one of them. "Brian, I sure hope you catch those punks. Do you think they picked her house at random?"

Brian's mouth formed a tight, thin line. "No. This wasn't a random act."

My heart sank into the pit of my stomach. I had a feeling what was coming next. And why was Brian staring at me? I tried to remain calm and picked up Cookie's rattle from the floor. "Why would someone do this intentionally?"

The bright green of Brian's eyes reflected off the light from the chandelier as he handed me a Ziploc bag. "Don't open it, Sally. It's evidence."

Through the clear plastic I could easily see the message someone had printed with a black Magic Marker, and I sucked in some air.

Tell Your Daughter To Butt Out, Or You'll Be The Next One Lying In A Casket.

CHAPTER TWELVE

————

My mouth was as dry as a piece of unbuttered toast. Everyone gathered around me to read the message, then their gazes automatically moved to my face.

"Oh no," Gianna murmured.

"Oh yes," Brian shot back.

Mrs. Gavelli gave him an incredulous look. "I no snoop. I *never* snoop."

"You lie, old woman," Grandma Rosa retorted. "But that message was not meant for you."

Mrs. Gavelli wagged a bony finger in my face. "What this mean? You set my house on fire, missy?"

"This isn't Sal's fault, Nicoletta," Gianna said. "She didn't want to be involved in the search for Eddie's killer in the first place." She narrowed her eyes at our father. "Sal was dragged into this."

"It's my guess whoever did this got the houses mixed up," Brian cut in.

My father threw up his hands in protest. "But Sal was happy to do it. She always helps everyone. Baby girl, why didn't you say something?"

"She did try to tell you." Mike's face was stern. "I believe I know what you're getting at, Jenkins. You think that someone is threatening Sal, and to get even with her, they decided to cause destruction to her parents' house. Only they picked the wrong one."

Brian nodded solemnly. "Exactly." His phone beeped, and he stared down at the screen. "Sally and Mike, I sent Adam over to check on your house. He said that everything looks fine. I'm almost one hundred percent convinced this incident has to do with Eddie Phibbins' murder. Unless, of course, you're working on another case I don't know about?"

I wasn't in the mood for Brian's sarcasm. Furious, I squared my shoulders against him. "No. I'm not. And for your information, I've been trying to stay out of this, but now it looks like I don't have a choice."

Mike groaned and sank wearily into a chair. "Great. I knew this was going to happen. Someone's made this personal, Sal. Why does it always happen to you?"

The room was silent as we all mulled his question over. No one appeared to have an answer.

My father took a sip from his coffee, frowned, and then added more anisette. "It's her fate. Hey, we all have one, right? Mine is to study death in all mannerisms. No big deal, son. It's not like Sal has been going around bothering people. We only made a little visit to Wally's house today after my breakfast meeting with Arthur. Then Sal and Josie chatted with Charlene, the cosmetologist. Nothing to worry about."

I loved my father dearly but wished that he would stop talking. Mike's eyes flashed angry blue sparks as my father continued rambling. Dad always had a knack for saying the wrong thing at the right time.

Brian placed his hands on his slim hips. "Wally is the guy that Eddie fired for stealing from him, correct? Domenic, why would you go to see him and meet with Arthur when he's at odds with his brother, one of your good friends?"

"Is there no end?" Mike wanted to know.

My father gave Brian a noncommittal look. "Arthur asked for me personally. He wants to advertise on my blog when he buys the funeral home from Linda. He's positive she'll sell it to him."

A vein bulged in Brian's neck. "How interesting. Is there anyone else that you and your daughter have talked to? Might as well enlighten me now."

"No one," I cut in.

"Sal's right." Dad helped himself to more tiramisu. "Oh, wait a second. You and Josie talked to Zach, right? That old bugger is as dedicated to the place as you can get."

Cookie was fussing, so Mike lifted her out of her bouncy

seat. "I think she needs to be changed," he said to no one in particular. Before I could say anything, he headed upstairs with the baby.

All I wanted to do right now was scream in frustration. Mike was furious, that was plain to see, and I honestly couldn't blame him. I'd dug myself a shallow grave so to speak and didn't know how to get out. Good grief. Now I was coming up with puns too.

Nicoletta finished her drink and rose, pointing a finger at Brian. "So if I no go home, what I gonna do?"

"Stay with Ronald," Johnny said quickly as he poured himself a glass of wine. He glanced at Gianna, who was finishing her third one, and then sighed and pushed his glass in front of her. Someone needed to drive home, and she was in no shape for it. We all knew what was coming next.

Mrs. Gavelli's eyes widened in amazement at she looked at her grandson. "Shame on you. What you think, I some tramp? We no married. I stay with you and Gianna."

The entire room went silent, waiting for Johnny to respond. My sister raised Johnny's glass of wine to her lips and then glared at him, waiting for him to say something—*anything*. The tension in the room was so thick you could have cut it with Grandma Rosa's antique cake server. Having Nicoletta under the same roof as Gianna was like striking a match against the side of a box.

Johnny's face turned a brilliant shade of crimson. "Um, maybe you'd rather stay here, Gram, with the Muccios. I mean, you'd be right next to your own home, if you need anything." He gave my parents a pleading look. "Dom, Maria, you've got plenty of room, right?"

"Nope." My father shook his head cheerfully. "Not for the spawn of Satan."

Nicoletta shook her fist at him. "I no want to stay here with this *pazza* anyway."

"Domenic's not crazy." My mother reached out to run a hand over my father's balding head. "He's so sexy and intelligent. Why, I never know what he's going to do next."

Gianna almost spilled her glass of wine while Johnny suppressed a cough. If there was ever a couple who was perfectly matched for each other, it had to be my parents. They both lived in a fairy tale world.

"It a wonder that Rosa still sane. Everyone here is *pazza*." Nicoletta grabbed her handbag off the table and shook it menacingly at Johnny. "I be in your car," she said. "You no keep me waiting."

Gianna gritted her teeth together as Johnny removed Alex from the high chair and put his coat on him. Alex waved bye-bye as Gianna poked Johnny in the arm. "Why didn't you tell her no?" she asked. "You know that she's impossible to live with! No one knows that better than you!"

Johnny lifted Alex in his arms and stared back at her. "What else is she supposed to do? Go to a hotel?"

"No hotel would have that old broad," my father declared as he chewed his cake.

Gianna's shoulders slumped in defeat, and after a moment, she grabbed her purse. "Fine. But she better not try to order me around!"

"You're a dreamer, my precious girl," Dad laughed.

"Domenic," my mother said gently. "I think you should stay out of their discussion."

Gianna picked up the diaper bag and whirled to face my father. "And as for you, Dad," she hissed. "You should have let the police handle the investigation. Now, because you insisted that Sal snoop into Eddie's death, you have Mike upset with her and the Sicilian version of the Wicked Witch of the West staying in my house. Will I *ever* get any peace?"

"Hmm," my father mused. "Just slip a little Benadryl in her drink, sweetheart. It will knock her out for a few hours."

Johnny touched Gianna's arm. "It's just for a few days, sweetheart."

Gianna leaned down to give me a hug. "Hang in there, Sal. Mike will understand."

Too bad I lacked her confidence. "Never mind about me. What are you going to do?" I wasn't sure who had it worse right now, me or Gianna.

"Say a prayer for me," Gianna whispered in my ear.

"That you survive?" I asked.

"No. That I don't kill her."

* * *

I bathed Cookie when we got home and then nursed her. For once, luck was on my side, and she fell asleep quickly. An evening with my parents was exhausting at any age.

After I'd laid Cookie down in her crib, I went into the bathroom to wash my face and brush my teeth. I glanced sideways into our adjoining bedroom. Mike was lying in bed shirtless, watching television, a can of beer on the nightstand beside him. His gaze met mine, and after staring at me for at least a minute with no comment, he returned his attention to the television. I shut the door to the bathroom and gripped the sides of the basin with a sinking feeling. Somehow, I needed to make this right and let him know I hadn't intended for this to happen. But how?

The red nightgown was still hanging on the back of the bathroom door, lonely and forgotten. I'd never gotten a chance to put it on the other night. With a sigh, I quickly undressed and slipped it over my head then shut off the bathroom light and went into our bedroom. As soon as I got into bed, Mike clicked off the television then rolled onto his side, away from me.

The action stung like a wasp, and I reached out to touch his shoulder. Thankfully, he didn't pull away. "Please don't be mad at me, sweetheart. I didn't mean for things to wind up like this."

He didn't answer.

I leaned over him so that I could see his face. "Will you please look at me when I'm talking to you? Don't shut me out."

Mike gave a sigh and flopped onto his back, pinning his dark blue eyes on me. "Okay, Sal. Tell me why I should listen when you don't give me the same courtesy?"

I tried to blink back tears but was unsuccessful. "Mike," I blubbered. "I'm so sorry. My father asked me to help him. How would you feel if a friend of yours was killed like that? I had no idea it would turn into this, but I couldn't tell him no."

A tear dripped off my chin as Mike watched. "Come here," he said gruffly and pulled me against his chest.

I continued to sob as he wrapped his arms around me.

"I'm sorry."

"No, princess. I'm the one who's sorry. I didn't mean to be such a jerk. But you've got to understand where I'm coming from. I'm sick and tired of seeing you always caught up in dangerous situations. Cookie needs you." His voice was soft against my hair. "And so do I."

I wiped at my eyes. "I don't know how to get out of this. All I wanted to do was help, and now it's backfired on me. If we don't find who did this, maybe something else will happen—to you or Grandma Rosa this time—"

"Stop it," he said gently. "Listen to me, baby." He wiped underneath my eyes with the pad of his thumb. "Let's see if we can figure this out together. You must be getting too close to the truth and have talked to the killer. Who can you narrow it down to?"

"In my opinion?" I sniffled. "Either Linda, Arthur, Wally, or Charlene." Zach crossed my mind, but I didn't feel his name was worth mentioning.

He ran his hands up and down my bare arms. "I wish I could fix this, but I know you won't back off now."

"I can't," I said in a choked-up voice.

Mike sat up in bed and placed his arms around me. "This happens far too often, Sal. I don't know why or if I can ever learn to accept it. Cookie needs a mother."

"She loves you more." The words flew out of my mouth before I could stop them.

He watched me in amazement. "Where is this coming from?"

"I don't know," I admitted. "She cries whenever I hold her but smiles for you all the time. She even looks just like you. It sounds crazy, but maybe I'm a little jealous."

He barked out a laugh. "Sal, you're her mother. She wouldn't be here if it wasn't for you. Don't you ever notice the way her eyes light up when you walk into the room?"

Mike's eyes were shining, and my heart melted into a puddle. Cookie did look at me the same way, with the same beautiful eyes that I never tired of seeing. "Maybe I didn't make the connection before."

He smiled tenderly into my eyes. "She's not smiling at

you like that because of gas, or because she's hungry, princess. It's because she loves you. Same as me. You two are the most important people in my life."

Tears started to gather in my eyes again. "Same here."

Mike sighed heavily. "I love how you put everyone else before your own needs. You make the world a better place and are the kindest and sweetest woman alive. But I have a confession to make. Some days I get tired of your family interfering in our lives. Well, except for your grandmother. I swear that woman is a saint."

"I wish I was more like her." Grandma Rosa always gave sound advice and knew how to fix everyone's problems. "Lately I feel so overwhelmed by everything and that I can't take proper care of Cookie, the bakery, or even you."

He gave me a teasing smile. "All in that order?"

I swatted his arm playfully. "You know what I mean."

Mike glanced at my nightgown and whistled. "Well, that's a good way to start taking care of me. You look gorgeous."

The way Mike looked at me when he said those words instantly made me feel better. He wouldn't care if I'd had a complete makeover or was wearing baby spit-up on my shirt. Mike loved me unconditionally, and that was all that mattered. "I've been neglecting you."

"It's okay, my love." He looked at me hopefully. "We both have a lot on our plates right now and need to spend more time with each other. Maybe even do a date night every week. But we're definitely having more alone time, starting this minute."

"Sounds good to me." I pushed him down onto his back and kissed him with renewed force. He chuckled and ran his hands through my hair.

"I do love it when you're feisty." He grinned. "Things will work out. We love each other, and that's what counts. You're an amazing mother to Cookie, and I'll help in any way that I can."

"That's why I adore you, Mr. Donovan." I pecked his lips.

"And I love you more than you'll ever know." Mike's expression turned serious as he gazed into my eyes. "Remember, it could always be worse."

His words sent a chill through me. "You mean, like being a suspect in a murder?" I didn't wish that on anyone.

"More horrible than that."

I drew my eyebrows together, wondering where he was going with this. "Being the victim?"

Mike grinned at me wickedly. "Nope. Not even close."

"I give up."

He chuckled. "You could be Gianna, and have Nicoletta living with you."

"Oh, so true." I wrapped my arms around him as he placed a trail of kisses down my neck. "It doesn't get much worse than that."

CHAPTER THIRTEEN

———

"Are you sure it's not in the house somewhere? Or maybe the bakery?"

"Positive, Sal. I must have lost it at Phibbins Mortuary when we dropped off the cookies to Linda."

I suppressed a groan. It would be nice to limit my trips to the funeral home, but it looked like that wouldn't happen anytime soon.

"Fine." I laid aside the batter I'd prepared for raspberry cheesecake cookies and removed my apron. "Let's go now and get it over with."

Josie looked at me in amazement. "You want to leave Dodie in charge again? On one of our busiest weeks of the year?"

"Well, I'm not about to let you go alone, especially after the incident at Nicoletta's house last night. Dodie will be okay by herself." *I hope.*

"Did you call me, girls?" A cheerful voice rang out from the storefront, and a moment later, Dodie Albert appeared in the doorway. She was a sweet-tempered woman in her sixties, with short silver hair sticking out from underneath her pink Sally's Samples ballcap. Although congenial and always anxious to help, it often wasn't the type of help we needed. Dodie had an unfortunate habit of making more work for us. Clumsy came to her as easily as dead bodies did to me.

"At your service." She grinned and stuck out her hand. It connected with the metal bowl of batter I'd just prepared, sending it up into the air and then crashing down on the floor. Pieces of the dough splattered Dodie in the face. She stumbled for a second, but I caught her before she collided with the cookie racks standing next to the oven.

I helped to steady her. "Are you okay?"

Dodie looked a bit dazed as she adjusted her apron. "All good. Not a scratch on me."

"I wish I could say the same for the cookie batter," Josie muttered under her breath.

With Dodie's help, we began picking up the mess. She grabbed a broom from the back corner, and I ducked as she swung it around in the air. "I'm so sorry about that, girls. What did you want to see me about?"

Josie raised an eyebrow, as if daring me to go through with it. "Yeah, what did you want to see her about, Sal?"

Fortunately, it was late morning and not a busy time. With a little luck, we'd be back within the hour. "We were wondering if you'd watch the shop for a little while. Josie and I need to run an errand. No need to do any baking. As a matter of fact, why don't you just stay in the storefront until we get back?"

Dodie's face brightened at my words. "Oh, of course! Now you two just go ahead and do whatever you need to. I'll take good care of the place."

"It's like giving someone permission to start a fire," Josie remarked as we got into my car. "Thankfully the bakery is doing well, but Sal, we may have to cut our losses at some point."

I placed the car in drive, and we moved down the alley. "But she's such a dear, and the customers adore her. I keep hoping that she'll get better."

Josie settled back against the seat. "You're forever the eternal optimist. Forget about that for now. Finish telling me what happened last night after you and Mike talked things out. From the smile on your face, I can wager a guess. Now the big question is will Cookie have a baby brother or sister in nine months?"

My face heated. "Will you ever learn tact?"

She grinned. "You should know better than to ask something like that. So I take it that everything is fine between my two favorite lovebirds again?"

"Yes, but I do understand where he's coming from." I put my blinker on and made a righthand turn into the funeral home parking lot. "We'll look for your bracelet and then clear out. I don't care if Linda's there. No chitchat. No cookie deliveries. And no more hanging out with dead bodies. But I would like to talk to Eddie's son if possible. He may have something to add. My father's trying to get ahold of him but hasn't had much luck, given the time difference."

"You'll figure this out. I have faith in you. Maybe you should think about writing a book," Josie suggested as we walked up the front steps.

I barked out a laugh. "Like my father? Don't you remember high school? English was my worst subject." The rest hadn't exactly been a breeze either.

"True," she admitted. "You and Mike were always skipping class. Remember that time Mrs. Bentley caught you two making out in the home economics room?"

"You were no angel either," I reminded her.

Josie grinned and opened the unattended front door. "What fun would that be? Okay, we'll get you a ghost writer for your autobiography."

I blinked. "Who would want to read *my* autobiography?"

She shrugged. "Why wouldn't they? It certainly can't be like any other one out there. Plus, if you sold some books, it could help to pay for Cookie's college. Rob and I are already trying to save for the boys. Do you know how high tuition is—"

"Can I help you, ladies?"

We whirled around in surprise. Zach was coming from the direction of Linda's office and looked anything but pleased to see us.

I gave a small wave. "Hi, Zach. Josie thinks she might have dropped her bracelet here last night."

He narrowed his eyes. "I always check the floors at the end of the night, miss. There is no bracelet here, I can assure you."

What was his problem? "Do you mind if we take a quick look around?"

He cocked his balding head to one side and studied me carefully. "Mrs. Donovan, I'm curious if this bracelet even exists."

"What?" Josie blurted out. "Of course it does. I'll show you a picture."

He looked unconvinced. "Is this some type of pretense to look around or, pardon me, to *nose* around like always?"

Someone was testy today. I smiled pleasantly at him. "I'm sure if you ask Linda, you'll see that she's fine with us being here."

"Linda's not here this morning. She went to meet with Arthur."

My heart gave a little jolt. "She's decided to sell the funeral home to him?"

Zach gave a casual shrug. "It's not for me to comment on such things. I try to mind my own business, unlike some people."

"What's the deal with you?" Josie demanded.

He gave a snicker. "The deal, you say? Are we playing cards?"

"Your problem," Josie answered. "Your beef. Isn't that slang for traditionalists like you?"

I poked her in the side. "Let's find your bracelet, and then we'll get out of Zach's hair—uh, I mean way."

Josie winked at him. "Maybe he's hiding something, Sal. Or he knows more about the murder than we think."

"Stop it," I hissed.

Zach's mouth tightened as he addressed Josie. "I have nothing against *you*, madam." He then pinned me with an accusatory stare.

Oh brother. I blew out a sigh. "What have I done now?"

"Honestly," he muttered. "This is too much. Throwing yourself at Nicoletta's boyfriend wasn't enough. Now you've tried to destroy her house? I never thought you'd stoop so low, madam. Why, you're—you're a shameless hussy!"

Josie snorted back a laugh, and I would have chuckled too, except it wasn't really funny. Zach's face was the color of a ripe tomato. This whole incident had gone too far. "Did Nicoletta tell you I tried to destroy her house?"

He shook his head. "No, Ronald did."

"What?" I gasped. "Why would he say something like that?"

Zach folded his arms across his chest. "Because you've been throwing yourself at him, of course. Ronald's always been quite the lady's man. Lucky for you, Nicoletta doesn't believe it.

She said that you're happily married with a new baby. Oh, and that you're crazy like the rest of the Muccios."

"Sounds like the old lady has a heart after all." Josie grinned. "Or at the very least, it does manage a beat from time to time."

I shot her a death glare. "This is all your fault. If you hadn't made up that dopey story to begin with—"

She choked on a laugh. "Okay, I'm sorry. Sal's telling the truth, Zach. I did make it all up."

He turned up his nose. "Don't waste your time defending her, young lady."

We'd already wasted enough time on this insane topic. "Can we get back to Linda? You really have no idea why she's gone to see Arthur?"

To my surprise, Zach's face fell, and he bit into his lower lip. "I'm worried," he confessed. "If she sells the place, I may no longer have a job."

How quickly things changed. A minute ago, I'd felt like smacking Zach upside the head, and now I was filled with genuine sympathy for his plight. "I'm sure that won't happen. You really like working here, don't you?"

He gave another noncommittal shrug. "It gives me something to do. Fills the day, so to speak."

"Maybe Linda's gone to see him about another matter," I suggested. "When she comes back, why don't you talk to her and see—"

Bam! The sound of glass shattering pierced my ears. I looked over at the entranceway and saw pieces of the front windowpane go flying through the air. Zach dove to the floor and just missed being hit by one. My eyes focused on a large black object that had landed near the podium and was smoldering away on the antique rug.

Terror coursed through my veins. This was a repeat of what had happened at Nicoletta's last night. "Oh my God! Is it a bomb?"

"Get back, Sal!" Josie screamed as she rushed toward it.

CHAPTER FOURTEEN

———

"What are you doing?" I shrieked and tried to grab Josie's arm. "We need to get outside!"

Zach quickly raised himself from the floor and ran past us, knocking into me. I lost my balance and fell as he rushed by for the door, not even looking back to see if I was okay. Chivalry was indeed dead, and Zach must have figured he wasn't far behind.

Josie was standing next to the blackened spot, watching it burn its way into the carpet.

"Get away from it!" I screamed.

"Sal, it's okay," she assured me. "It's not an M-80. Looks like a regular firecracker that someone attached to a rock."

"How do you know? And who did this?" Too late, I ran to the front entrance and flung open the door. Shards of glass that had been clinging to the remnants of the windowpane fell on impact. I peered outside into the parking lot and street, but there was no activity. No guilty party running away from the scene or a getaway car zooming past us at 100 miles per hour.

"Damn," I cursed under my breath and rushed back to Josie's side. She was sitting on her knees, talking to a 9-1-1 operator.

"Yes, that's right," she said calmly. "At Phibbins Mortuary. No, we didn't see anyone. Yes, of course we're outside." She gave me a sly wink. "Okay, thank you very much." She clicked off. "Help is on the way. With our luck, it will be Brian."

The smoke had dissipated, but the air was acrid, and my eyes started to water. I squinted down at the object. "You're sure it wasn't an M-80 like the one at Mrs. Gavelli's?"

Josie snorted. "Not even close. Those can do a heck of a lot more damage. Didn't you ever set firecrackers off as a kid? Oh wait. I forgot who I was talking to for a minute."

I placed my hands on my hips. "And I suppose you did?"

"Oh sure. My brothers always had them." She got to her feet and looked around the room. "What happened to our buddy after he shoved you out of his way?"

"At the rate Zach moved, he might be all the way to Canada by now." I stepped outside onto the porch and scanned the surrounding area. His car was still in the lot. "Zach?" I called loudly.

A hand shot up from behind the well-kept evergreen shrubs. I crossed over to the tree and helped the elderly man up. After a few seconds, Zach had steadied himself with my support. He flicked a branch off his head and stared at me sheepishly.

"Are you all right?" I asked.

He nodded, his Adam's apple bobbing in time. "I'm sorry, miss. I guess I panicked."

"It's okay," I assured him. "We were all scared."

His clear blue eyes searched mine. "It must have been the same person who killed Eddie. They're trying to scare us all off."

"We don't know this for certain." But I silently agreed with him. First Mrs. Gavelli's house and now the funeral home. A jolt of fear shot through me as realization set in. I'd been the only person present at both places. This was no coincidence. Someone wanted to make sure I minded my own business.

Sirens wailed in the distance. Zach and I watched as a firetruck pulled into the parking lot followed by a police car. I cringed when Brian and Adam emerged from the vehicle. Good grief. Weren't there ever any other cops on duty in Colwestern?

Two firefighters nodded as they hurried past us. Brian was talking to someone on his phone. He looked up, and our eyes met. He didn't look happy to see me. This wasn't going to end well.

I decided to beat him to the punch. "We didn't do anything wrong. And there's no fire. Josie told the 9-1-1 operator on the phone, so they're wasting their time."

He lifted his eyebrows. "They have to check it out either

way."

Without further comment, he held the door open then followed Zach and me inside. For a second, I was foolish enough to believe that would be the end of it, but after a quick word with the firefighters, Brian grabbed me by the arm and pulled me into the viewing room.

"Let go!" I tried to wriggle free, but he was having none of it. He slammed the door shut and then whirled to face me. His green eyes had darkened, and I could visualize smoke pouring out of his ears.

"Tell me this," he seethed. "Why is it that disaster follows everywhere you go?"

Josie opened the door. "Okay to come in?"

"Yes," I said.

"No," Brian growled.

"It's not her fault," Josie said quickly. "We came here to look for my bracelet. I think I dropped it—"

He threw his hands up in the air. "Just stop. It's always something like that with you two. I was foolish enough to believe you'd stay out of this and mind your own business after what happened at Mrs. Gavelli's house last night. I should have known better. You two can't keep your noses out of any murder investigation in this town. While we're at it, don't you have a business to run?"

Josie glared at him. "Don't worry about the bakery. It's in good hands." She crossed her fingers behind her back.

Brian's nostrils flared. He reached down, removed his badge from his uniform shirt, and then held it out to me. "Here you go. It's obvious that you and your friend here think you can do a better job than the police at finding Eddie's murder, so please, feel free to take over."

The action shocked me. Sure, Brian had been ticked off at me for interfering in prior investigations, but he'd never behaved like this before. Everyone had their limit, but he needed to understand where I was coming from.

"How do you think *I* feel?" I shot back. "I didn't want to be involved in Eddie's murder. I was only going to ask a few questions to help my father. I promised Mike I'd stay away from investigating after Cookie was born, and guess what? There's no winning for me! I'm like the Pied Piper of dead bodies because they follow me everywhere. Now someone is targeting me, and I have no choice but to be involved."

"Sally." Brian gritted his teeth in exasperation.

"No!" I pointed a finger at him. "You're going to listen."

Josie was visibly impressed. "You tell him, girl."

I blew out a breath and tried to calm myself. "I'm not trying to do your job. Believe me, I happen to have plenty of faith in you and the police department. You've saved my life more than once, remember. But don't tell me to walk away because it's too late for that. So perhaps we can find a way to help each other and somehow get justice for Eddie. Is that okay with you?"

"Don't be so hard on her." Josie put an arm around my shoulders.

Brian sighed in resignation. "All right. Tell me exactly what happened when you arrived today."

I gave him the quick, condensed story. As I was finishing up, a tap sounded on the door, and Adam came in followed by Zach.

"I just questioned him." Adam nodded at the elderly man. "He said he ran as soon as the firecracker came through the window."

"I didn't know he could move that fast," Josie remarked.

Zach's face flushed. "Do you think that whoever threw the firecracker is the same person who killed Eddie?"

Brian gave him a strange look. "We can't be sure, but it's a possibility."

"I see." The elderly man seemed uncomfortable. Josie shot me a questioning look. Did Zach know more than he was letting on?

Brian watched us, his eyes narrowed. "First Mrs. Gavelli's house. Now the funeral home. What do *you* think this means, ladies?"

"That someone dislikes Mrs. Gavelli and funeral homes?" Josie teased. "But there's a lot of people who fall into that category."

The color rose in Brian's neck.

"She's only kidding," I said.

Brian folded his arms over his chest. "It's bad luck on Mrs. Gavelli's part that she lives next door to a certain Italian family. Would you agree?"

"Oh fine," I grumbled. "Yes, someone's angry that Dad and I have been asking around about Eddie's death."

"Very good," he mocked. "I'm glad to see that you're paying attention here."

I snapped my fingers. "Wait a second. Maybe whoever did this wasn't intentionally trying to do damage to the funeral parlor."

Brian shot me a puzzled look. "What do you mean?"

"Josie told me so herself. The M-80 at Mrs. Gavelli's could have burned her house down. But this was a standard firecracker. What if whoever tossed the firecracker through the window was just trying to scare us and not cause a lot of damage here?"

Brian mulled this over. "Good observation. You may have a valid point."

"What's going on?"

We turned around to see Charlene standing in the doorway. She was dressed in all black with a wide brimmed hat, full-length black leather coat, and matching boots. It was the perfect wardrobe for a funeral. Her eyes were puffy and red, as if she'd been crying.

"Miss Jones. Where did you come from?" Brian asked.

Charlene looked confused. "I came in through the back of the building like I always do. It's nearest to my work area." She glanced around at us. "What's going on? There's no wake today, but I do have a body to prepare. It's always nice to have an audience."

"Someone threw a firecracker through the front window," Brian explained. "Do you know anything about it?"

Charlene stabbed a finger into her chest. "Me? Why would I know anything about it? What are you implying, Officer?"

"I'm not implying anything," Brian said calmly. "I wondered if you might have seen anyone suspicious on your way in."

"Oh." Charlene blushed. "Sorry, I shouldn't have jumped

to conclusions." She looked around the room again. "Is Linda here?"

"Zach said she went to meet with Arthur." I turned to reaffirm this with Zach, but he'd slipped out of the room.

"He's outside talking on his cell phone," Josie said.

"Then it's true." Charlene's face hardened. "She really is going to sell the place to him. I can't say I'm surprised, but I won't work for that man. He's a sleaze. Nothing at all like his brother."

Brian edged closer to her. "Do you think Arthur could have been responsible for his brother's death?"

Charlene wrinkled her nose as if a putrid smell had invaded the room. "I didn't think so before, but now I'm not so sure. He just wouldn't let up on Eddie. And Linda's weak. She never liked the business and didn't give a damn about Eddie's feelings. Yesterday she—" Charlene hesitated and didn't finish the sentence.

Brian latched on to her reaction. "Is there anything else you'd care to tell me?"

"I heard Linda on the phone with someone last night. She thought I'd left but I had to come back for my sweater." Her eyes sparkled with mischief, as if she had a secret. "She was crying and everything. I heard her tell the person on the other end of the line that she didn't have it and begged them to understand."

"Have what? Money?" Josie mused out loud. "Maybe she owed someone dough? Or it could have been a bill collector."

"It all fits," I said. "She needs money badly, so she's selling the place to Arthur. I hope she at least gets a fair price."

Charlene bit into her lower lip. "Personally, I hope she gets zilch. Nada. A big zero. Eddie had a heart of gold, and she stomped all over it." She hoisted her purse over her shoulder. "Now if you'll excuse me, I have a friend waiting."

After Charlene had left the room, Josie rubbed her arms as if for warmth. "That chick gives me goosebumps. Maybe it's just me, but the way that she calls a dead person her friend is creepy."

"Charlene was trying hard to make Linda look like a

viable suspect," I remarked.

Brian leaned against the door. "What are you getting at, Sally?"

"I'm not sure," I confessed. "She hated Linda and adored Eddie. We know that Charlene was carrying a torch for him, so would she really do away with him?"

"Maybe they were carrying on," Josie proposed, "and he refused to leave Linda for her. She got angry and killed him."

"My father insists that Eddie wouldn't do such a thing. Wally also said that Eddie had resisted her advances. So why lie about it?"

Brian's shoulders sagged. "All right, I wasn't planning to tell you this, but we got Eddie's autopsy back yesterday."

"Were you able to find anything? I asked. "I was under the impression that the embalming might have messed with the results."

"It's always a possibility, but luckily, no, not in this case. We learned that Eddie died from cyanide poisoning. It was something he either ate or drank. Cyanide works more quickly than any other type of poison. Eddie would have been dead within minutes of ingesting it."

"The killer watched him die." An icicle formed between my shoulder blades. What type of lunatic were we dealing with? The world could be a dark and evil place, but I still held on to the belief that most people were good. It was upsetting how these psychos always found their way to Colwestern. Even worse was realizing that the person who had killed Eddie was someone he had worked with at one time or another. A person he had trusted.

"We're going to find the person who did this." Brian looked at me, as if guessing my thoughts. "Sally, I know that you won't leave this alone, so I'm asking you to please be careful. Someone would be only too happy to place you inside a coffin as well."

CHAPTER FIFTEEN

———

Gianna reached for another fudgy delight from the plate in front of her. It was her third one in the last fifteen minutes, a clear indication of how agitated she was.

"I don't know how much more of this I can take, Sal," she confessed as she licked the fudge frosting off the sugar cookie's surface. "She's driving me bananas. I got up at three o'clock in the morning to get a drink of water and found her in the kitchen rearranging my cabinet shelves."

I sipped my hated decaf. "You knew this was going to happen. Nicoletta could drive Mother Theresa crazy."

"Truth." Gianna nibbled around the cookie's edge and made her way to the center. "Do you know what else? She said that Johnny looks like a walking skeleton. It's obvious that I'm starving him to death. Nicoletta said he's lost weight since we got married because I don't know how to cook."

"Sweetheart, you know that I love you more than anything. Believe me, Nicoletta drives me crazy too, but she's right. You *don't* know how to cook. Neither do I for that matter."

Gianna's jaw locked in a determined manner. "Well, I can make hamburgers. And I made macaroni and cheese the other night."

I raised an eyebrow. "Nuking a box of Stouffers doesn't count."

"Oh whatever." She reached for another cookie. "Give me some credit. I'm trying."

I leaned back in my chair. The sun was in full glory this morning, its beam of light shining through the bakery's front window and basking me in its warmth. I had convinced myself that the bright, cloudless blue sky was a good omen and nothing bad would happen today. No more dead bodies, no fire bombings, and no sightings of Mrs. Gavelli. The last one pertained to me but not my sister.

"I think it's great that you're trying, but Nicoletta's talking about real cooking. Lasagna, pasta e fagioli, braciole. The dishes that you and I can only dream about cooking someday while she and Grandma can make them blindfolded." No one could match our grandmother in the Italian cuisine department, but Mrs. Gavelli was probably a close second.

Gianna swallowed the rest of her coffee in one gulp. "Nicoletta told me that she was making dinner tonight and wouldn't take no for an answer. I don't like anyone ordering me around in my own home, but when she told me what she was making, I caved." She blew out a sigh. "I sold out for stuffed peppers."

I patted her hand. "Hey, I would have done it for a frozen cheesecake." My phone buzzed, and I glanced down at the screen. Our parents' landline. "Hello."

"Hi, sweetheart." My mother gave a halfhearted giggle in my ear. I raised an eyebrow at Gianna's questioning stare and whispered, "Mom."

She rolled her eyes in return.

"What's up?" I asked.

Mom paused for a second. "Your father is on his way over to the bakery. He's determined to get to the bottom of who killed Eddie and needs your help, darling. Please don't disappoint him."

"I'll do what I can."

She blew out a shaky breath. "Sweetheart, I'm really worried about him. He's not himself these days. He only had one piece of your grandmother's cheesecake this morning."

Okay, this was terrible, but my main concern now was not that Dad had only consumed one piece of Grandma Rosa's cheesecake but the fact that I hadn't been invited over to sample any. I sincerely hoped there were leftovers. "Maybe he wasn't feeling well."

"No," she insisted. "There's more. He can't—" She paused again.

Oh, good grief. If this had anything to do with their love

life, I might lose my breakfast. "Mom, it's okay. You don't have to tell me."

Gianna shot me a questioning look, but I shook my head at her.

"He can't blog." My mother hiccupped back a sob.

"What do you mean he can't blog?"

Mom released a long, pent-up breath into the phone, as if she'd been holding it for an eternity. "He can't write. That's how much Eddie's death is affecting Daddy. He can't do what he's always been meant to do. His heart just isn't in it anymore."

Gianna groaned out loud. "Gee, the world will come to an end if Dad can't blog."

I lifted a finger to my lips and hoped my mother hadn't heard her. "He'll be okay. I'm sure it's just a temporary thing."

"I wish I could believe that," she sighed. "But it's a daily ritual for your father. Why, he's so organized. The first thing he does in the morning, after he has breakfast and a piece of pie or cake, is to sit down with his coffee and write his daily blog. Then he tweets, Instagrams, and posts to his Facebook author page. Why, Daddy's followers look forward to his unique thoughts. When there was no blog yesterday, they started panicking. They began messaging him, worried that he was ill."

I stared at the phone in disbelief. Who were these people? Okay, I would understand this behavior if we were talking about J.K. Rowling, but not my father. Yes, he'd written a book and self-published it, which was admirable, but 99 percent of his sales had come from the Colwestern community itself. He called himself a bestselling author and compared himself to Stephen King when he was about two million copies short. He claimed that our town loved him and that his book was unique. The latter was definitely true. My family always gave the town grapevine fresh dirt to thrive on.

"I'm sure he'll be fine, Mom. Maybe he just needs to take a breather. Everyone has to take a break now and then."

"Well, I hope so," she sniffed. "I just put the baby down for a nap. She's such a little angel. Sweetheart, your grandmother wants to talk to you. Why don't you and Mike come for dinner tonight? She's making lasagna."

"We'll be there." I hated myself for asking this. "Is there

any cheesecake left?"

There was a muffled sound on the other end as my grandmother came on the line. "But of course there is. How are you, *cara mia*?"

"I'm…managing." That was an understatement. "How's Cookie?"

"She is sleeping. She had a bottle of milk and some cereal and went out like a bulb."

"That's light, Grandma."

"Whatever. The solids will make her sleep better, *cara mia*. But only a little cereal for now. In a few weeks, you can try some of my applesauce."

"As long as I get some too." Grandma's homemade applesauce, like everything else she made, was amazing.

"But of course," she replied.

"Thanks for watching Cookie today." I clutched the phone tightly between my hands. "Grandma, Mom and Dad seem to be acting a bit weirder than usual."

"That is not possible," she said. "They cannot get any weirder."

"Is everything okay?"

My grandmother grunted. "Those two are regular *pazzas*. What if your papa cannot blog? Oh, the world is certain to end."

"I can't believe he has so many people depending on his posts," I mused.

"What can I tell you?" Grandma Rosa asked. "I do not understand it either. The world has gone to hell in a wastebasket."

I had to stop and think about that one for a minute. "Um, I think that's handbasket, Grandma."

"That is good too," she agreed. "Your papa should be there shortly. I am glad. I need a break from that man. Your papa is worried about Eddie's legacy. He said that Linda wants to talk to him privately about the funeral home's future. He would like you to go with him."

"It's really none of our business what she decides to do with the place."

"Yes, I know this. But try to tell your father that."

I said goodbye and clicked off. Gianna was talking to

Josie, but they both stopped and looked over at me.

"Let me guess," Gianna said. "Dad can't function as a blogger again until he finds Eddie's killer."

I reached for one of Josie's cappuccino cookies, already having forgotten my earlier resolution to diet and exercise today. The cookies were a new creation of hers made with one teaspoon of coffee and cocoa powder, rolled in sugar for an extra sparkle. I was craving coffee like crazy, and every little bit helped. "Something like that."

Gianna shut her eyes. "Just when I think he can't get any weirder."

Josie waved her wrist at me. The tiny rubies sparkled off the sunlight streaming through the window.

"You found your bracelet!" I said excitedly. "Where was it?"

She sat down at the table and removed it from her arm, then placed it in a small box. "Under the back seat of my van. It must have fallen off when I put Robbie in his car seat."

"I'm so glad you didn't lose it."

We all sat there for a minute, enjoying the peace and quiet. My bakery had been bustling all morning and Josie and I were glad to be off our feet during the temporary lull.

Josie propped her hands up on her elbows. "What's your latest guess about Eddie's killer?"

I willed myself from grabbing another cookie and sipped my bland coffee. "It has to be one of the five people associated with Phibbins Mortuary."

"Because Eddie was embalmed," Josie remarked.

Gianna shivered. "The whole thing grosses me out. It's so morbid."

"The wife is always the main suspect," Josie pointed out. "But Linda didn't know how to embalm."

"Also, what did she have to gain from Eddie's death?" I asked. "He left her the funeral home, which she never wanted to run, and now she's in the process of selling it to Arthur. Who knows if she'll even make her money back?"

"There must be special stipulations in the will," Gianna mused. "If a business owes money or a potential lawsuit is pending, you can't go ahead and sell it till that's been resolved.

So I'm guessing Linda's trying to pull a fast one before those lawsuits rear their ugly heads."

It would make sense. "Personally? My bet is on Arthur. He had the biggest motive to kill his brother—greed. He's been salivating for years to get his hands on the place. As for Zach, he was angry about being demoted, but he was also with us when the firecracker came through the front window."

"In my opinion, they all seem to be missing a few screws," Josie said. "What about that Wally character who was ripping Eddie off?"

Gianna snickered. "You have to love the guy's philosophy. He steals from his boss, puts the urns up for sale on eBay, and then says Eddie ruined his life because his wife left him. And we think Dad is strange."

Could Wally have become so enraged that he killed Eddie for pressing charges? It was possible. The same with Zach. I'd seen other people kill for less of a reason.

"Last but not least, we have Charlene Jones. She denies the rumors about fooling around with Eddie, and Dad claims there's no way Eddie would do that to Linda. Charlene was much younger, but some women like older men."

"Much older men in her case," Josie added. "Eddie was at least twenty years older than her. And it's not like he was a sugar daddy. He was sorely lacking in the asset department."

"All that may not have mattered to her." Charlene had clearly adored her boss, but had she killed him for resisting her advances? Or had Linda found out about an affair and done away with her husband in anger?

The bells on my front door jingled, and my father stepped into the bakery. He was dressed in a Sally's Samples navy blue sweatshirt, tan-colored shorts, white tube socks, and brown leather sandals. He rubbed his hands together in satisfaction. "Three of my favorite girls. Josie's like my third daughter, you know."

Josie smiled warmly at him. Sure, she thought my father was a nutcase and was often vocal about it, but deep down I knew she was fond of my parents and vice versa. My mother and father had done more for her growing up then her own parents had. She stared down at his legs and whistled. "Nice outfit,

Domenic. Isn't it a little cold for shorts?"

"Nah." He snatched a jelly thumbprint cookie off the plate and patted Gianna on the head. "We're supposed to have an early summer, so I'm getting started now." Dad sat down in the chair to my left. "Baby girl, how about going to pay Linda a visit with me?"

"Sure thing. But Dad, you have to understand, if she wants to sell the place, that's her right. This isn't any of our business."

He furrowed his brow. "I know she needs money, but I owe it to Eddie to try to talk her out of it. Business is bound to go back up eventually. She needs to weather out the storm, so to speak. I mean, people die every day. Someone in this town is bound to drop dead today or tomorrow."

"Really, Domenic," Josie gasped.

Gianna shuddered. "Dad, you say the sweetest things." She stared out the front window in interest as a bleached blonde alighted from a black BMW. "Oh good. She's right on schedule."

I shielded my eyes against the sunbeam for a better look. "Who's that?"

We all watched as the woman approached the bakery. She looked to be in her late thirties or early forties and had a spectacular curvy figure. Despite the lukewarm day, she was dressed in a white linen blouse and a denim miniskirt so tight and short that it made the ones my mother wore seem respectable.

My father lowered his gaze. The woman's legs were long and shapely, bare and ending in a pair of red designer pumps with at least a four-inch heel. Sighing, I returned the fudgy delight cookie back to the plate in the center of the table.

Dad looked momentarily flustered. "Nice-looking lady. Seems to me I've seen her before. Of course, she can't hold a candle to your mother."

"She should look familiar," Gianna answered. "That's Chantal Jones."

I stared at my sister in amazement. "Are you talking about Charlene's twin sister? Why is she here?"

"Because I think she might be able to help us find Eddie's killer."

CHAPTER SIXTEEN

———

I had to wonder about my sister's motivation to bring Chantal to my bakery. She was a lover of the law and would never do anything that might compromise her position. "Okay, but I still don't understand why she would agree to come here."

"Chantal thinks I asked her to come and discuss the recent charges that were brought against her, even though the case was dismissed," Gianna explained. "She was fired from Jerry's Juice Bar, and the owner hasn't offered her the job back. Chantal, in turn, wants to file a suit against Jerry, which I plan to talk to her about. But the real reason I asked her here is so you could question her about Charlene." She narrowed her eyes at our father. "But I hadn't planned on anyone else being here."

"That was great of you to stick your neck out." I was certain Gianna had another reason for doing this.

Gianna lifted her chin in defiance. "I know what you're thinking. Yes, I want Nicoletta out of my house as soon as possible, and I'm not ashamed to say so. But I'm also doing this because I'm worried someone in my family might get hurt next." She watched me solemnly. "Namely you, Sal."

My father raised the cup of coffee in his hand that Josie had brought him and saluted Gianna. "Well done, sweetheart. Everyone has to get a little devious where Nicoletta is concerned."

"Damn straight," Josie agreed.

"Just follow my lead," Gianna said. "Chantal might have useful information to add about her sister—something we don't already know. They're not exactly close, even though they live together, and they've got to converse at some point. Maybe we'll find out that Charlene and Eddie were having an affair."

My father shook his head. "No way."

Chantal stepped into the storefront and looked around the room, seeming not to notice us. Her eyes were focused on the contents in the display case.

Gianna went to her. "Thanks for meeting me here, Chantal."

She nodded and stared at all of us with unabashed curiosity. My father rose and patted his chair. "Please, take my seat."

"This is my father, Domenic Muccio," Gianna said as way of introduction. "My sister Sally, who owns the place, and her head baker, Josie Sullivan."

We all exchanged a round of hellos. "Can I get you a coffee, Miss Jones?" I asked.

She raised an eyebrow. "No thanks. Have we met before?"

Oh crap. Gianna hadn't said her last name yet. "Uh, no. Gianna told us who you were when you got out of the car."

She seemed to accept this and snapped her gum as she sat down. My father stood next to her, making no attempt to move away. Chantal gave him a flirty smile and crossed one lithe leg over the other in a seductive manner. I was impressed. Her skirt was so tight that I wasn't sure how she'd pulled off the maneuver without splitting it in two.

Gianna frowned up at our father, who seemed frozen in place. "Dad, there are more chairs if you'd like to sit down."

"I'm fine right here, sweetheart." He grinned.

Jeez Louise. "Can I get you something to eat, Miss Jones?"

"Call me Chantal," she murmured in a low, husky voice. "Maybe a fortune cookie. I do love those silly things."

"Me too!" my father said jovially. "Sal and Josie make the best ones. It's a blast to read the messages because they come true. Why, these cookies are more accurate than the weather report."

Josie went behind the counter and returned with a plate of fortune cookies that she set in front of Chantal. She snapped one open immediately and laughed as she read the message inside. "It says, 'Honesty is your best policy.' How cute!"

That's what we were hoping for.

Chantal turned her attention back to Gianna. "Jerry's been in touch since I last spoke to you. He said that if he hires me back, the rest of the girls have threatened to quit. They're just jealous because I was the best earner. I mean, he doesn't have a choice, right? And I need that job."

Gianna frowned in reply. "It could mean another court case, if you're okay with things dragging out a bit. How about we go pay him a visit later this week?"

She looked at my sister in amazement. "Really? I had no idea you'd do something like that for me."

"I'm always willing to help." Gianna paused. "By the way, your twin sister works at Phibbins Mortuary, doesn't she?"

Chantal popped a piece of fortune cookie into her mouth and groaned. "These are so good. They practically melt in your mouth and are way better than those stale ones in the Chinese restaurants."

Josie's face brightened at the compliment. "Thank you."

Gianna tried again. "Charlene is a cosmetologist, right?"

"Yeah, Charlene works on dead dudes. What a freaky occupation, right? Then again, she's always been a little strange. Terrible shame about what happened to the owner, though."

"Our father was good friends with him," I added. "He's very broken up about his death. What an awful way to go."

"Yeah," my father broke in before I could stop him. "The girls were wondering if your sister was carrying on with Eddie."

Josie groaned and Gianna cursed under her breath. If looks could kill, my father would be with Eddie right now.

Chantal didn't seem too put out by his question. "Charlene's always liked them old. *Real* old in his case." She winked at my father. "I mean, he's got to be as ancient as you, sugar."

Ouch. That had to hurt.

My father's chest deflated at her words. "Hey, I'll have you know that my wife says I'm in my prime, and she's 13 years younger than me. Why, she says I've got the stamina of a—"

"Dad, please!" I interrupted. "Chantal, I've met Charlene. She seems very nice."

Chantal glanced down at her fingernails, painted black

with silver glitter. "Yeah, she's okay. Too nerdy for my taste. We've never been close. People always think that, just because you're a twin, you've got to be attached at the hip or something. We also don't approve of each other's career choices. But hey, at least I make good money at mine."

Double ouch. Chantal might bring in more cash, but I wasn't sure if she could walk and chew gum at the same time.

"I thought you two lived together?" Gianna asked.

She shrugged. "Yeah, with our mother in my house. It's more of a matter of convenience than liking each other, though. I pay all of Mom's bills while Charlene pays squat. She doesn't make a lot of money at the dead people place. I think she only stayed because she had a crush on the old man. He was awful tight with the buck. Charlene thought they were having financial troubles, but that struck me as kind of odd." Chantal picked up another fortune cookie and sniffed it.

Chantal struck *me* as kind of odd. "Why would you say that?"

"Because when our father died last year, we held his wake and funeral there. Charlene even did his makeup."

I gave an involuntary shudder while my father grunted in satisfaction. "She's a good girl. So nice that she'd do that for her old man."

"Don't get any ideas," Gianna warned him.

Chantal snapped open the cookie and read its message. "Ha! This one says, 'Beauty is in the eye of the beholder.' It's almost as if the cookies know we're talking about Charlene."

I was tempted to throw the other two away but restrained myself. "You said you thought it was odd that Phibbins Mortuary was having financial difficulties."

She nodded vigorously. "My father didn't have any life insurance, and Eddie only gave Charlene a ten percent discount on the funeral. That casket was way overpriced, if you ask me. The entire thing ended up costing close to ten grand. I should know because I paid for it."

Something here wasn't adding up. Phibbins Mortuary certainly had its share of customers. It was rumored that Eddie had been stealing from his clients. Was that to feed his gambling addiction? Funerals were expensive, and employees like

Charlene, whose talent for making people like Cady Perry beautiful, must be difficult to find. Yet she wasn't earning much money at it.

So where *was* the money going? Did Eddie still have a mortgage on the funeral home? "Did Charlene mention that there might be lawsuits against the place?"

Chantal chewed on a piece of fortune cookie. "Nope. Never. It wouldn't surprise me, though. I didn't trust the guy. He had shifty eyes. Charlene was all gaga over him, but I wasn't impressed. Oh, and Charlene hated his wife. From what she told me, the feeling was mutual."

My father shifted uneasily from one foot to another. Normally he delighted in any morbid gossip, but this was his friend we were talking about. If Chantal was telling us the truth, the case against her sister wasn't looking good.

"Charlene was close with Eddie?" Josie asked.

"I already told you, she had a crush on the old coot." She cracked another fortune cookie open and pushed the last one at me. "Here, you open this one."

"I'm good, thanks."

Chantal crunched on the cookie then smiled at my father, who was still glued to her side. "While you're up there, handsome, I've changed my mind. I'll take a cup of coffee. Black, please."

My father's round, pink face broke out into a full-fledged grin as he hurried over to the bakery case.

Josie went after him. "I'll get it, Domenic." I knew what she was thinking. Josie was afraid he might cause a sudden disaster. One Dodie in our bakery was enough.

Chantal winked. "Men always do exactly what I tell them."

Way too much information for me. "That's my father you're talking about."

Chantal looked nonplussed. "Oh, I didn't mean anything. It's just a job to me. But I do happen to be very good at it."

Gianna rolled her eyes. "Let's get back to your sister."

"Hey, what's with all the questions about Charlene anyway?" Chantal wanted to know as my father brought her coffee. "Oh, wait. I get it. You think my sister might have killed her boss, don't you?"

"Oh, no," we all cried in unison.

Chantal seemed disinterested in her sister's plight as she read her latest message. "'Don't give away all your secrets.' Hey, these are great. I'll have to order a bunch for my New Year's Eve party." She nudged me. "Come on, open yours. I insist."

Defeated, I cracked the cookie open.

"What's it say, baby girl?" My father leaned over my shoulder with interest.

I crumpled the paper up in my hand. "It says, 'Don't believe everything you hear.'"

Chantal giggled. "Well, you can bank on what I say because I don't lie. There's no reason for me to. Do I think my sister could have killed Eddie? Yeah, maybe, if she realized she could never have him. I think anyone is capable of murder." She thrust a finger at Gianna. "Haven't you ever thought about killing anyone?"

Gianna's face reddened. "Of course not. I'm a lawyer, remember."

"All the better reason," Chantal giggled.

An image of Nicoletta crossed my mind as Gianna blushed. "Okay, well, not seriously," she admitted.

Chantal rose to her feet. "Let me know when we can go see Jerry about getting my job back." She gave my father a playful little chuck under the chin. "When I'm back at the juice bar, you come see me, sugar, and I'll give you all the free drinks you can handle."

My father, in turn, gave Chantal his best "Aw, shucks" grin, waited until she'd departed, and then turned to me. "Come on, baby girl. Let's go see Linda. I'll drive." He rushed out the front door and was just in time to see Chantal blow him a kiss as she drove by.

"She's quite the character," I said.

"You're not kidding," Gianna muttered as her cell phone buzzed. She started chatting with someone while Josie went to wait on a customer. Ever the impatient soul, my father began beeping his horn for me.

As I gathered up my purse, I suspected that Chantal was telling us the truth. Her main concerns in life revolved around herself and money. She seemed disinterested in Charlene's plight and only worried about what she could lose—namely, her job as a topless waitress.

At this moment, I was more concerned about what *I* had to lose. When I'd opened the fortune cookie minutes ago and read the message aloud, I had lied to everyone in the room. A chill swept over me as I un-crumpled the strip of paper and stared down at it with a sinking feeling.

Don't wind up six feet under.

CHAPTER SEVENTEEN

———

"Why does Linda want to see us?" I asked my father on the drive over to Phibbins Mortuary. "It's not like she needs our permission to sell the place."

My father puffed out his chest. "She trusts my insight, of course. Seems reasonable to me. The poor woman needs someone to help her make decisions, especially since her son isn't around. Still, I think it's a mistake and know Eddie would be against it."

"But she needs money to survive, Dad."

He sighed. "Yeah, that is kind of important. Well, at least the place will stay in the family."

"Yes, but maybe with Eddie's killer running it."

Dad pursed his lips. "It's a grave matter, baby girl."

The parking lot was deserted, except for Linda's light blue station wagon. My father and I walked around to the rear entrance. "Linda should get a camera installed back here," he said. "I'll bet that's how Wally got away with stealing the urns. He came out the back way instead of the front so that he wouldn't be seen."

I struggled not to roll my eyes. "Gee, Dad, you're pretty good at this sleuthing thing."

"Darn right I am. It must run in the family." He reached for the knob, and it turned easily in his hand. He held the door open for me to enter first. "Maybe you should tell Josie that she's been replaced."

Linda must have heard us, because she was standing in the doorway of Eddie's office. Her thin face looked pale and tired. "Oh, I'm so glad it's you. Hello, Dom. Hi, Sally. Thanks for coming. Let's talk in the office."

My father and I seated ourselves in the plush chairs while Linda settled herself behind the desk. She twisted a ballpoint pen between her slim fingers. "I want to thank you both for all that you've been doing to try to help me find out who killed Eddie, but I just can't handle it anymore. I need to distance myself from the place."

"You don't have to explain anything to us," I said. "It's your business to do with as you please."

She smiled. "I appreciate that and thought I should tell you in person that I've decided to sell the funeral home to Arthur."

My father sucked in a loud, obnoxious breath, which I tried to ignore.

"Are you sure? It sounds like Arthur will be getting what he wanted all along. We don't even know if he's the one who—" I didn't finish the sentence.

Linda nodded her head adamantly. "I know I accused him before, but it was all in the heat of the moment. I refuse to believe he killed Eddie. We're talking about his own flesh and blood here."

My father and I said nothing.

Linda must have taken our silence for disbelief. "What other choice do I have?" she cried abruptly. "I need the money, and he's offered me a fair price."

Why was she getting so defensive? Maybe Arthur had threatened her. "Does Eddie have any other assets that you could sell? What about waiting until someone else comes along to buy the place?"

"Eddie had nothing else, save the funeral home. The will isn't being read until later today. His attorney, Roger Dudley, has been out of town the past few days. He did inform me over the phone that Arthur will be present for the reading as well." Her face was pinched tight with worry. "That must mean Eddie left him something. What, I have no idea. It may have been his attempt at a peace offering."

I'd only been to a will reading once before, and the experience had not been pleasant. It hadn't been for a relative but a murder victim instead. The whole experience had left a terrible taste in my mouth as slighted family members slung more hateful words around than a roadside diner did with hash. But I was curious what Eddie could have left his brother. "Can you let us know the details afterwards?"

She shot me a puzzled look. "Why?"

"Maybe it's a motive for Eddie's death."

"Oh." Her face fell. "That makes sense. If it helps, I've seen Eddie's will before. He made it out shortly after he received the funeral home from his father, and I was a witness. The funeral home goes to me, but if I die, it passes on to Terry." Her brow furrowed. "I don't remember Arthur being named at all."

"Doesn't Terry have to be present for the reading?" my father asked.

Linda shook her head. "Roger contacted him directly, and he's asked that we proceed without him. If I remember correctly, Eddie left him some personal items. A gold watch that belonged to his father and some other trinkets. He might be a little upset to know that he isn't getting cash—then again, there isn't any."

I made a mental note to ask Brian to check out Terry's records and see if he'd made any recent trips to the US. Perhaps there was another suspect that I hadn't considered yet.

Linda came around the desk, and we took that as our cue to leave. "I hope you don't mind, Sally, but I've told Arthur about your fabulous cookies. He may be getting in touch."

"Of course not." Never mind the cookies. I still couldn't believe that Linda might be selling her husband's pride and joy to a possible killer. Money was a strong motivator.

My father took her hand between his. "I hope you know what you're doing."

"Me too," Linda said weakly.

"What will happen to your employees when Arthur takes over?" I asked.

"There's only Zach and Charlene to consider, and Charlene has already stated she plans to look for another job." Linda wiped at her eyes. "I do hope Arthur decides to keep Zach on, but it's not my problem anymore. To tell you the truth, I'm not sorry to see the last of him. Zach's been acting kind of strange lately."

"How can you tell?" my father said as I nudged him.

Linda's mouth turned up at the corners. "It might be best if Arthur starts with a clean slate."

As far as I was concerned, the entire funeral home needed a clean slate. Eddie's death would surely leave its mark on the place forever.

Linda exhaled sharply as she walked us to the door. "The truth will come out soon, I'm certain. The police were here earlier with a search warrant, but I don't believe they found anything."

We said goodbye and the door closed and locked behind us. Dad slung an arm around my shoulders and led me in the direction of Starbucks. "How about a mocha Frappuccino, baby girl? My treat."

"Sounds good, as long as it's a decaf." The word still sounded foreign to me, and I wondered if I'd ever get used to it. Probably not.

The heavenly aromas of cinnamon and roasted coffee beans wafted through the air when my father opened the door. This was my place, my people. I'd once worked as a barista for a Starbucks in Florida while married to my first husband, Colin. It had been a difficult time for me—trying to save a marriage that there was no hope of saving while also trying to forget my one true love. I'd been the one to support us financially and had worked over sixty hours a week just so we could get by. On the plus side, I'd made some good friends while working there, and fond memories rushed back to me now.

"I still don't understand," I said as my father gave our orders to the barista.

He looked at me quizzically. "What?"

"Charlene is very attractive. Okay, she likes older men. That's not unusual. But in most cases, the man has money or is drop-dead gorgeous." Sadly, Eddie was neither of those.

My father stared in surprise. "Baby girl, you know it's what's on the inside that counts."

"I do know, but I'm afraid not everyone thinks the same way."

He gave me a solemn look. "You're forgetting something. I'm thirteen years older than your mother. She's always been a knockout, while I'm just your average Joe. I didn't have any money when we met. She could have done way better than me."

"Well, you're special in your own way, Dad." So was my mother, which might explain both their mindsets. Whatever the reason, I was grateful they'd wound up together.

Dad stroked his chin. "I am, aren't I?" He paid for our drinks, and we walked back to his car. "Then again, so was Eddie."

"This has to be the most unusual murder case I've ever—" My phone buzzed, and Brian's name flashed across the screen. "Hi, Brian."

He cleared his throat. "Sally, I wanted to let you know that we've arrested Charlene Jones for the murder of Eddie Phibbins."

Boy, they worked fast. I put a hand over the phone and addressed my father. "Charlene's been arrested."

Dad nodded soberly. "Yeah, I saw it coming."

"But why? I'm not convinced it's her."

"Hello?" Brian's irritated voice boomed from underneath my hand. "Excuse me. I don't mean to interrupt your chat session, but could I have your attention, Sally?"

"Sorry. My father's with me. Why was she arrested?"

"We obtained a search warrant for the funeral home and found a vial of cyanide in her workstation. It was hidden in her cosmetic tray," Brian explained. "She swore she didn't know how it got there."

"That sounds too convenient," I murmured. "Charlene's not stupid. Why would she put it there?"

"She had a motive," Brian reminded me. "Everyone who was questioned said she had a crush on Eddie, but he resisted her advances. He also paid her a miserly wage for a job that requires a fair amount of talent. Not everyone can do what she does."

Or want to. "Do you think she's innocent?"

"It doesn't matter what I think. It's all about the evidence, and my job is to bring her in." He paused. "Of course, if she's not the one, it may catch the real killer off guard."

That had been my thought too.

"She's asking for a lawyer," Brian went on. "More specifically, she'd like Gianna to represent her. Can you locate her? Charlene said that Gianna recently represented her sister and comes highly recommended."

"Well, she is the best."

Brian ignored my comment. "Is there any chance you can find Gianna and have her down at the police station within the hour?"

My ego deflated a bit at his words. For a moment, I'd thought that Brian had called to take me under his wing so to speak, like a mother hen does to a baby chick. He'd shared details with me on cases in the past, but it looked like this time would be different. "Sure. I'll call and ask her, but I don't think it will be a problem."

My father, who had been listening in, already had Gianna on speed dial. He motioned to me with his phone and whispered, "Your sister said she'll go over now and wants to know if you'd like to tag along for the ride. She's only a couple of blocks away and will drive over to pick you up."

"Sounds good to me."

"Sally, are you still there?" Brian asked.

"Sorry. Yes, my father just spoke to her. We'll be there in about ten minutes."

A deafening silence met my ears. *"We?"* Brian echoed. "What's this *we* stuff?"

"I'm only going along for the ride, no worries."

He muttered something under his breath that sounded like a curse word. "And that's *all.* You'll wait by the front door until she's done talking to Charlene. Or in the car would be even better. Like normal people do, Sally."

What was that supposed to mean? "Yes, of course. I wouldn't dream of interfering. Has Linda been notified yet?"

"If you must know, she hasn't. We're trying to keep Charlene's arrest under wraps for a while, so I'm counting on you and your morbid father not to say anything to anyone."

I fumed at his remark. "Jeez, we're not two years old, Brian."

He grunted in exasperation. "Some days, I wonder. Sally, I swear, if you—"

"Gotta go. See you soon," I said sweetly and clicked off without another word. "Wow. What a grouch."

My father's eyes practically bugged out of his head. "Maybe Charlene really did kill Eddie because he wouldn't leave Linda. If he'd pretended to be interested in her, he might still be alive."

I had no answer for that.

"How about I go along with you and Gianna?" he asked hopefully. "Then we can all talk to Charlene."

If my father came along, Brian might toss us out into the street. "It doesn't work that way, Dad. You'd have to wait out front, like me. Anyway, you've got a more important job to do. You need to keep Charlene's arrest top secret. The police are counting on you."

I didn't think he'd buy it, but Dad nodded eagerly. "Sure. I'll be a regular Sherlock Holmes. You and Mike are coming for dinner tonight, right? We need to discuss our next step in the investigation."

Yes, I'd created a monster.

My phone beeped with a text from Mike. *I need to finish this kitchen tonight. Will be late. Save me some dinner? Then when we get home, maybe my beautiful wife and I can pick up where we left off last night?*

His words warmed me from head to toe as I typed out, *Totally. Can't wait.* I added several hearts and smiley face emojis.

I shielded my eyes against the sun and spotted Gianna's car approaching. At least my husband and I were back on the right track. And our precious daughter was safe, basking in the glow of her grandmothers' love. My thoughts returned to the fortune cookie message I'd received, and I couldn't help but wonder about my safety as well.

CHAPTER EIGHTEEN

———

As Gianna drove toward the police station, she chatted gaily about the new words that Alex had learned to speak. I made appropriate replies and tried to be attentive but was lost in my own little world.

Was there someone else who'd been involved in Eddie's murder that I hadn't accounted for? Another person who had access to the building and also performed embalming? The scenario had me baffled. Someone had poisoned a well-respected mortician, embalmed him, and then placed him in one of his own coffins. Before they could dispose of the body, they'd taken off and left him in his funeral home, where my father had been the one to stumble upon the body. He must have interrupted the killer before they could finish the job. The killer must have known there were no wakes scheduled for that day and assumed they were in the clear.

Or had they meant for Eddie to be found like that? Was the killer trying to frame someone else, like Charlene? And what about Terry, Linda and Eddie's son? Could he have come home and killed his father? But what was his motive? England was only seven hours away by plane. Although Terry was out of the country, he couldn't be discounted.

"You're awful quiet," Gianna said observed. "Everything okay?"

I pulled out my phone and dashed off a message to my father, asking if he could try to reach Terry again. "Fine. But I'm not convinced Charlene did this. Doesn't it seem a little too obvious to leave cyanide in your makeup table? As far as I know, it doesn't cover blemishes."

Gianna almost smiled. "After what I see in the

courtroom daily, nothing surprises me anymore."

"Not to put you on the spot, but is there any way I could talk to Charlene as well?"

"You know better than that." Gianna scolded me like I was a five-year-old.

Hey, it had been worth a shot. I said nothing further as she pulled her car into the adjoining lot next to the one-story, gray brick building. I'd visited the police station several times over the past few years—actually, too many to count. The last time I'd been here, Brian had joked about getting me my own parking space.

I tried another tactic. "If Charlene doesn't mind, would it be okay then?"

Gianna's brown eyes narrowed as she shut the engine off. "Sal, it nulls the attorney-client privilege. I'd never agree to anything like that."

"But if she agreed, you'd be okay?" I persisted.

"Yes, but I would never ask her. And why would she agree to it when she barely knows you? The whole thing is unethical. I couldn't get behind something like that. You know I believe in total honesty."

"Well, you did ask Chantal to come to the bakery, and you weren't exactly truthful about it," I reminded her.

Gianna lowered her eyelashes and sighed. "You're right. I'm a hypocrite. A dishonest attorney."

"No, you're not! I was only teasing. Besides, you had your reasons."

Her face was grim. "I need that woman out of my house before I go insane." She slammed the car door with renewed force. "What kind of attorney am I? What example am I setting for my son? Will I turn the other cheek every time my child does something wrong?"

Good grief. "Gi, I didn't mean to sentence you to a lifetime of remorse. If this is going to upset you, I'll stay out front. Promise."

She sighed and linked her arm through mine as we walked into the station. "If you can get Brian and Charlene to agree, it's all right by me."

Brian was in conversation with the man stationed behind

the front desk when we arrived. He spotted us and immediately walked over. "Thanks for coming, Gianna. I'll bring Charlene into the interrogation room, where you can chat with her privately."

"Brian," I interrupted. "Is there any chance—"

"Forget it," he snapped and turned away.

So much for that. Resigned, I sat down on the hard, wooden bench that was located against the wall while Gianna looked at me sympathetically. "Sorry, Sal."

"No worries. Maybe you can find out if she and Eddie really were carrying on."

"I thought you said she denied it."

"Yes, but there's always a chance she's lying." I snapped my fingers. "Hey, could you get your hands on a copy of Eddie's will?"

Gianna looked doubtful. "Has it been read?"

"No. Not until sometime this afternoon."

She frowned. "I wouldn't be able to check it out until it's a public record. We don't even know if it has to go through probate. If there's still money owing on the funeral home, that's a given. Do you know who the attorney or executor is?"

"Linda said his name is Roger Dudley."

"Oh, sure. I know Roger. We've been in court together a few times. I'll contact him. He may give me some information after it's been read."

While we were speaking, a door down the hall opened, and Charlene came into view. She was dressed in a hunter green shirt and matching pants with her wrists cuffed in front of her. Brian had placed a hand under her elbow and guided her toward the interrogation room. Charlene's eyes locked on me and then Gianna. She exhaled sharply, as if she'd been holding that one breath for an eternity. Brian didn't even glance our way. After a few seconds, he reappeared in the doorway and motioned to Gianna. He closed the door after she'd entered.

"Don't you have to stay in there with them?" I asked.

He shook his head. "She's allowed to have a private talk with her attorney. Besides, we have visual monitoring without audio."

The door to the interrogation room reopened, and

Gianna gestured at Brian. "Can I have a word with you?"

He walked over while I shot off a text to Josie, letting her know I'd be back at the bakery within the hour. She responded right away, saying Dodie was there and they'd be okay until I returned.

Brian came back over to me, shaking his head in disbelief.

"What's wrong?" I asked.

He pinched his nose between his thumb and forefinger. "It appears that Charlene has requested your presence. Gianna swears she had nothing to do with it."

"Are you serious?"

"Unfortunately, yes," he said dryly. "For some odd reason, Charlene believes you can help her too."

"I'll do my best." Before Brian could say anything further, I rose from the bench and walked into the room, shutting the door quietly behind me. Gianna motioned for me to sit at the table next to her.

Charlene stared at me with a somber expression. She looked like she'd aged since the last time I'd seen her. There were strands of gray in her hair I was certain hadn't been there before.

"I didn't do it," she blurted out. "You both have to believe me. I adored Eddie."

Gianna's face was unreadable as she tapped a ballpoint pen on the table. "Who could have planted the cyanide in your room?"

"Anyone. The door is never locked. I supposed a mourner could have come in, but that's doubtful. You have to believe me," she insisted. "I never would have hurt Eddie."

"The last time I spoke to you when Josie was with me, you asked us to leave your work area," I remarked. "You became upset when she asked if you were carrying on with him."

The room grew silent, and I found myself wondering if Brian was watching us.

It seemed like an eternity before Charlene spoke again. "We weren't carrying on. I would have liked to, but he rejected my advances. I tried to get him to kiss me once in his office. Linda walked in while I had my arms around him."

That explained why Linda thought they'd been having an

affair. "What happened then?"

"She said I was a tramp." Charlene's nostrils flared. "Linda and Eddie started arguing, and she called us both filthy names. I was terrified and ran out of there. The next day, when I showed up for work, Eddie said it would be best if we kept our distance. He started acting very strange, but not only to me. He was that way around everyone." Charlene threw her shoulders back in defiance. "I know he was twenty years older than me, but I didn't care. Age is just a number."

"No one's judging you about that. But he was a married man," I said.

"Yes but not happily," Charlene sniffed.

Gianna had her lawyer face on, devoid of emotion. "If I'm going to help you, Charlene, you need to be honest with me."

Charlene's cuffs clanked against the table as she clasped her hands together. "I'm telling you the truth. Someone else killed him, and my money is on Arthur. He planted the cyanide in my room and is getting what he's always wanted now that Linda is selling him the funeral home."

"Do all of the employees know how to embalm?" I asked.

She thought for a moment. "Arthur does, of course, and Wally. But not Linda. Zach used to do it for his former employer, I believe."

"How long ago was it that Linda caught you and Eddie together?" Gianna asked.

"A few days before he died." Charlene bit into her lower lip. "I was positive Linda would tell Eddie to fire me, but nothing ever came of it. She chose to ignore me instead. Then again, she was always good at that. I know she was jealous of me."

Gianna changed the subject. "Did you know about the funeral home having financial problems?"

"Someone mentioned it to me," Charlene said. "But I'm not really sure how that's possible. The place is popular, so that never really made sense."

"People have complained about jewelry being stolen off the deceased," Gianna explained. "Their loved ones."

Charlene's jaw went slack. "How horrible. I'd never dream of doing something like that."

"But you had access to the jewelry?" I persisted.

She shook her head. "Personal possessions are always the first thing to be removed—before embalming, before anything. I've done embalming, but only in situations where no one else was available. The body doesn't come to my station until afterward. I can't believe Eddie would do something like that. He was an honest man."

Someone was lying, but who? I was certain that the families who'd brought the claims against the funeral home were telling the truth. Gianna had said there was more than one pending.

"May I ask a question?" Charlene asked timidly.

Gianna nodded. "Of course."

"When can I get out on bail? I'm not going to have to spend the night here, am I?"

Gianna's face was sympathetic. "I'm afraid so. This isn't a misdemeanor. You've been charged with murder. You'll have to go before a judge."

Charlene looked panicked. "I can't stay here!" she wailed.

"I'll do my best to get you out as soon as possible," Gianna promised. "Now is there anything else you care to tell me?"

Charlene paused to consider. "The day before Eddie disappeared, I went to his office to ask him about ordering some supplies since we were getting low. He was sitting behind his desk staring into space. This was weird because he was always doing something. The man was never idle. He didn't look well, and at first, I thought he was sick. So, I asked him what was wrong, but he said nothing."

"And then?" Gianna prompted.

She swallowed nervously. "Eddie always downplayed everything. He never wanted anyone to worry about him. He was the consummate professional, always concerned for everyone else. His clients, staff, and family. Sure, he was tight with the buck, but we all knew that was just his way. That day was different. Eddie didn't act like himself. He looked like he'd just lost his best friend. Even the piece of paper he was holding in his hand was shaking."

"Did you happen to see what it was?" I asked curiously.

Charlene shook her head. "It looked like a legal document, but I couldn't say for sure. When I came closer, he shoved it into his desk. Then he told me to leave and acted kind of nasty about it too. It upset me so I quickly left the room. A few minutes later, I remembered that I'd totally forgotten to ask him about the supplies. Eddie was on his cell and had his back to me. He sounded like he was crying."

Gianna and I exchanged a puzzled glance. "Did you catch any of the conversation?" she asked.

Charlene wrinkled her brow and stared into space. "It was something like 'I saw it.' No wait—'I found it.' Then he asked the person on the other end, 'How could you do this to me?'"

CHAPTER NINETEEN

———

Josie stared down at the tray of sugar cookies she was decorating. They were a perfect replica of Easter eggs in pastel colors of pink and green. "What I don't understand is why Charlene didn't tell the police about Eddie's phone call. It could be the key to his death."

"She said she didn't make the connection before." I removed another tray of sugar cookies from the oven and placed them in the baker's rack to cool. We'd been working our bunny tails off all day long, so to speak. The holiday was only two days away, and many customers had waited till the last minute to place their orders.

"Next year, we're cutting orders off at least five days ahead of time," Josie announced as she carried the tray of cookies to the waiting display case. "Getting back to Eddie. That comment of Charlene's seems kind of strange. Did you and Gianna tell Brian about it?"

"Of course, we told Brian. I mean, it was the least I could do. He could have been a jerk and not let me into the room to talk to her."

Josie rearranged the trays to make more space. "But Charlene did ask for you."

"Yes, but I happen to understand where he's coming from. And I'm not about to start hiding information from him that could help the police do their job, especially when my family's safety is a concern."

Josie returned and began to frost a tray of bunny ears with buttercream icing then arranged pink glittery sprinkles on the inside part to accent them.

I watched in admiration. "They look perfect."

She grinned. "Thanks. Mrs. Alden ordered two dozen of the ears. She wants to hide them for her children to hunt instead of eggs. Those kids will be bouncing off the walls from all that sugar. Hey, to each her own, I guess."

I tapped my fingers against the metal tray, trying to figure out my next move. "What do you say we do a little poking around in Eddie's office and see if we can find that document he was holding when Charlene last saw him?"

Josie's face lit up like the sun. "Sure, but you don't even know what it was. He probably has lots of legal documents in his desk. It might be like looking for a needle in a haystack, Sal."

"You're right." I snitched a cookie that Josie had finished decorating and bit into it. The frosting was sugary sweet, addictive, and satisfying. "But it's worth a try. I'm not sure where else to go with this."

Josie switched decorating tips and went to work on designing squiggly lines for the Easter egg cookies. They were perfect, like everything else she did. I felt guilty standing there and munching on cookies while she did all the work, but that didn't stop me from eating another one.

"Do you want to ask Linda about the document? Maybe she'd know what it was."

I grabbed a paper towel and dabbed at my mouth. "Dad said she's out of town today. Something about visiting friends in New York City."

"Okay, so you can't talk to Linda, and Charlene is still in jail. What about Zach, Wally, or Arthur?" Josie suggested.

"I've already talked to everyone. If one of them is Eddie's killer, they're not going to be sharing any more information with me. From what Charlene said, someone did a terrible thing to Eddie, and he was awful upset by it. Maybe he decided to confront the person, and then they killed him."

"With cyanide," Josie reminded me. "He ate or drank something that had the powder in it. Which also means he knew his killer…well."

The monitor on the worktable came to life, and a shrill cry broke through the room. I wiped my hands on my apron. "Sounds like someone's up from her nap. I'll be back in a few."

Josie waved me off. "Take your time. Cookie's more

important, and I can handle things here for a while. Now, if we can close at five, we'd have enough time to run over to the funeral home and do some more snooping. Rob's off tonight and we're going out, but not until seven o'clock."

"Aw, how cute," I said teasingly. "It's so nice to see old married couples still in love, having a date night."

"It's really more of a let's grab a quick burger and get stuff for the kids' Easter baskets while we have a free minute," she quipped.

I took the wooden stairs two at a time to the small apartment above the bakery. It was under a thousand square feet in size but cozy and comfortable, with a combination kitchen and dining area, one bedroom, and a small living room. Cookie was on her back in the travel Pack 'n Play, her plump legs kicking at the air furiously. Her sweet little face was scrunched up and red from exertion. I reached down and gently gathered her into my arms, giving her a light kiss on the forehead. "How's my sweetheart? Hungry?"

She kept fussing as I laid her on the nearby dresser and quickly removed her soiled diaper. I felt so fortunate to be able to bring my daughter to work with me and that I had this area at my disposal. Not everyone had the same luxury. Today probably wasn't an ideal day to bring her in since we were so busy, but she'd been at my parents' most of the week, and I wanted her with me.

As I sat in the recliner to nurse Cookie, I basked in the solace, which was occasionally interrupted by the sound of bells announcing a customer below and familiar voices calling greetings to Josie. If things got crazy, she would yell for me, but I was enjoying this special time with my daughter. Josie was right. Cookie was more important than any sale, and I had to treasure these moments while they lasted.

The apartment had been many things over the last few years. Gianna had lived here for a time after a fire had destroyed my previous bakery location. When she'd moved out, a friend of Mrs. Gavelli's had run a business for a brief time before she met her unfortunate demise. Then my father had stepped in, hosting a book signing for his death novel and followed that up with teaching a class on blogging. We could use the money a potential rental would bring in, but I was glad that we'd chosen to let it remain vacant for now.

As I stroked Cookie's soft cheek, a wave of anxiety passed over me. What else might Eddie's killer have in store for me or my family? Should I even go back to the funeral parlor? It might not be safe, but Josie would be with me, and we always had each other's back. Besides, it wouldn't take long to search Eddie's office—if I could get inside. Zach was usually there, so I might have to make up some flimsy excuse. It would be easier if there was a wake in progress, but I doubted Linda would have left town then.

I burped Cookie then brought her downstairs in her bouncy chair. Josie was waiting on a customer with one hand and had the phone in her other. Cookie and I headed into the back room, and Josie joined us there shortly. She began decorating another tray of cookies.

"I'll be here by five tomorrow morning," she announced. "We just got two more orders for Easter egg cookies and another for a basket of assorted cookies while you were upstairs. Dodie promised that she'll be here all day to help, and Mickey's booked solid for deliveries in the morning. He can give us a hand in the afternoon if needed."

"Sounds good to me. Thanks so much for keeping everything running so smoothly. I don't know what I'd do without you." I gave my daughter a rattle shaped like a yellow bird to hold, and she rewarded me with a toothless grin. It was her favorite toy to play with. I sat cross-legged on the floor, lightly rocking the chair back and forth. The brightly colored toys attached to the handle moved back and forth in time with it.

"No worries, hon. I've been in your shoes, and I know what it's like." Josie smiled down at Cookie, rattle in hand. "Hey, that reminds me." She reached under the cabinet by the sink for her purse. She removed a small gold box and handed it to me.

"What's this?" I asked, mystified.

Josie tossed flour and eggs into the electric mixer. "I picked it up for Cookie last night. I know she's already got a ton of these, but I couldn't resist. Consider it an early Easter present from Aunt Josie."

I lifted the lid on the box. It was another rattle to add to

Cookie's collection, but I'd never seen one like this before. The plastic handle was blue and attached to an Easter Bunny head of cloth-like material. "Aw, it's adorable. Thanks for thinking of her."

"Press the button in the center of his forehead," Josie commanded.

I held the rattle in my hand and did as she instructed. A bright, intense light shone directly in my eyes, forcing me to blink several times. "Whoa! Holy cow, that thing is blinding!"

Josie's forehead furrowed as she bent down next to me. "Jeez, I didn't think it was that powerful. Sorry, Sal. I can return it for something else."

I pressed the button again, facing the light away from Cookie. She giggled and held her hand out. She began to fuss again, so I let her hold it. "Well, Cookie seems to like it. I'll see if I can find some way to disconnect the light later."

"She's not crying much today." Josie said thoughtfully as she stared down at my daughter. "See, I told you it was only a phase."

Cookie dropped the rattle, and I shoved it into my jeans pocket. She stuffed her fingers in her mouth, so I quickly whipped up a small bowl of cereal then spooned some into her eager, waiting mouth. "Grandma said that she should be having solids."

"She's a big baby," Josie observed. "At least twenty pounds. It's not unusual to start babies on cereal at her age."

"Well, it seems to be working," I admitted. "The last couple of nights, she's been sleeping better. But she wants to nurse less." This made me sad, and I hoped the end wasn't in sight, because I enjoyed the bonding time with her.

"You've given her a great start," Josie said. "It may only be a temporary thing, so don't worry. Look on the bright side. Once she starts taking a bottle full time, you can return to being fully caffeinated again."

I'd momentarily forgotten about that part. "I think giving up caffeine has been more difficult than childbirth itself."

Josie laughed as another customer entered the store. "I'll get that," she said and disappeared while I wiped Cookie's face with a burp cloth. I gave her the yellow bird rattle to play with as

I washed my hands and went to work on batter for thumbprint jelly cookies.

Josie returned, wearing a puzzled expression. "There's a man here to see you. He said his name is Arthur. Isn't that Eddie's brother?"

I almost dropped the mixing bowl. "What the heck does he want?"

She shrugged. "He said he'd take two dozen coffin cookies to go and then asked if you were around. He seems nice—go figure."

"Maybe he's been cloned." I put Cookie's chair on vibrate and stepped out of the room.

Josie stood in the doorway with one eye on Cookie and the other on me.

Arthur was dressed to the nines in an expensive black suit and loafers that had been polished until they shone. He was staring intently into the display case but looked up when I came in and then gave a gallant bow. "Well, look who's here. Nancy Drew in the flesh."

"Did you come to insult me?" I tried to keep my voice at an even keel, but it took some effort.

He laughed good-naturedly. "Aw, that was just a joke. Look, I'm sorry about the other night. Let's start over, shall we?"

His new and improved attitude wasn't fooling me. The man was up to something. "What can I do for you, Mr. Phibbins?"

"Call me Arthur," he said smoothly. "Look, since I'll be taking over the funeral home from Linda, I'd like to talk to you and your partner about catering some more upcoming receptions. On the average, I expect to have them two or three times a week. I believe you were giving Linda a discounted rate, and I'd appreciate it if you'd extend the same courtesy to me. This way we can all make a profit, right?"

I stared at him in disbelief. What was with this guy? First, he wanted to hire my father's blog service, and now he was looking to me for cookies? He'd practically threatened Linda into selling the place, and now that she'd finally agreed, everything was all sugar and no spice? "To tell the truth, Arthur, I'm a little surprised. You were a jerk to Linda and me the other night, and now you want *me* to help *you* make a profit?"

His face sobered. "I apologize for that. But you have to understand. That was before I knew that Linda would sell, so I was upset. Today is a new day. A day of celebration."

What did he mean by that? "I'm sorry. You're always welcome to order cookies at the regular price from us, but we won't be making any more trips to the funeral parlor."

"But you did it for Linda," he protested.

"That was different. Besides, I only did it because my father asked me to." I placed my hands on my hips. "I have to admit I'm curious what you said to make her sell the place. Why didn't she respect her husband's wishes?"

Arthur's eyes turned cold and dark like a cesspool. "Because she knew she didn't have a choice. The place is in the red, and I'll be the one to get it out. Although…" He hesitated.

"Go on," I urged.

"Eddie was always a good businessman, but somehow he managed to run the place into the ground." Arthur chuckled under his breath. "Sorry. A little funeral home humor."

I didn't feel like laughing. "What are you implying?"

Arthur proudly stuck his nose into the air. "Only that I'm better than Eddie. The place always did well, even when my father owned it. I don't know why there are losses being reported, but it doesn't matter. I've got enough money and am confident I can turn the place around."

"Can I ask what you do for income now, Mr. Phib—err, Arthur?"

He cocked an eyebrow at me. "Sure, you can ask. I have nothing to hide. There's money left over from my deceased wife's estate. I've made some good investments over time and am ready to sink some serious dough into the place. Sort of like what you do here—get it? Dough?"

Arthur must have thought I'd never heard that expression before. I smiled politely. "How long did Eddie have a gambling problem?"

He shrugged. "Oh, I'm really not sure. Linda told me about it. If you must know, we weren't exactly close the last few years, ever since our father died. I mean, we talked occasionally, but that was the extent of it."

"Did it surprise you to find out?" I asked.

He shifted from one foot to the other uncomfortably. "Sure. I mean, I guess. My brother was never the type to take risks before. He was all about the sure things in life. Eddie liked to play it safe."

Arthur's attitude on the subject was vague, and something wasn't adding up. Everyone seemed surprised that the funeral home had been in dire straits. No one knew much about Eddie's gambling problem or the theft of jewelry. My father had insisted that Eddie was an honest businessman, and Charlene had reiterated the same.

For someone who had always tried to play it safe, Eddie had been cheated big-time in the game of life.

CHAPTER TWENTY

––––––

My mother and Grandma Rosa were seated at the kitchen table when I dropped Cookie off an hour later. "Is Dad taking a nap in his coffin?" I asked.

My mother put down the Cosmopolitan magazine she'd been reading and refilled her coffee cup. "No. He's upstairs lying down because he's not feeling well. I hope it's not the flu."

Grandma Rosa, who was bouncing Cookie on her knee, grunted. "Perhaps it is the three pieces of cheesecake that he ate earlier. If that man had one more bite, he would have busted a move."

"I think you mean gut, Grandma."

She shrugged. "I like that too."

I placed two bottles in the fridge for Cookie when my father's voice boomed from up above. "Is that my baby girl? Both my baby girls?"

"Sal's getting ready to leave, sweetheart," my mother called and then turned to me. "Where'd you say you were going? I thought you and Mike were coming to dinner."

I hesitated. Even if my father wasn't feeling well, he still might want to tag along to the funeral home, and I preferred that it only be Josie and me. "To run a quick errand. Mike's working late, but he'd love it if you'd save him some lasagna. It will just be Cookie and me for dinner."

My father appeared in the kitchen doorway, holding a bottle of Pepto-Bismol in one hand and his cell in the other. His face was pale, and his eyes looked glassy. He held out his phone to me. "I think you'll want to take this."

"Who is it?" I asked.

"Terry Phibbins. Linda and Eddie's son. He finally

returned my call."

I took the phone from my father's outstretched hand and walked into the living room with him following. "Hello, Mr. Phibbins? This is Sally Donovan, Domenic's daughter. I'm sorry for your loss."

"Thank you," a deep male voice replied. "Forgive me, but I'm not really clear as to why your father keeps calling me."

"Dad was a friend of your father," I explained. "He's looking into his death, and I'm helping."

There was a pause on the other end. "I thought Domenic ran some kind of morgue-related blog. My father mentioned it once. I didn't realize you were both detectives,"

"Actually, I'm—no, we're not. You see, I've been involved in a couple of murder investigations before, so Dad asked if I'd help him." A second too late, I realized how peculiar this must have sounded but continued rambling on. "I'm sorry you weren't able to make it home for your father's funeral."

"Look, Mrs. Donovan. If you must know, my father and I weren't close. I feel awful about what's happened, but my mother understands that I can't be there, and she's fine with it."

"That's not why I wanted to speak with you." It wasn't any of my business, but I couldn't fathom how an only child wouldn't travel home for his father's funeral, despite their differences. Nothing would have stopped me from making the trip. It was a matter of respect as far as I was concerned, but everyone might not feel the same way. "Are you close with your mother?"

Terry sighed impatiently. "Yes. We talk weekly. She and I aren't of the same mindsight as my father. We never have been. Mom can't stand the funeral business, and to be honest, it's always given me the creeps. Growing up, my dad worked side by side with my grandfather, and I was expected to help at times. Little things like opening the door for viewers, then watching him embalm and such. I hated everything about the place, and my friends always teased me to no end. I mean, how would *you* feel if your father drove you to school in a hearse every day? Oh, never mind. I'm sure you have no idea what it's like."

I glanced over at my father, who was downing half the bottle of Pepto-Bismol. "Try me. You might be surprised."

"I'm sorry?"

I wasn't going there. "Never mind. Mr. Phibbins, err, Terry, my father and I thought you might be able to give us information that would help determine who killed your father."

"Haven't you talked to my mother?" Terry sounded surprised.

"Yes. She thinks it may have been one of your father's employees, but no one's been able to prove anything. I wondered if you had some insight."

He was silent for a beat. "No, I don't. This has been a horrible experience for her. She only wants to sell the place and be done with it all."

"I can understand that, especially since it wasn't doing well."

"Wait a second. The funeral home is having money problems?"

"You didn't know?" I asked in disbelief.

"My mother never said a word." Terry's voice took on a suspicious note. "Why does my uncle want to buy the place if it's not profitable?"

I clutched the phone tighter in my hand. "That's what I was wondering. This sounds terrible, but do you think that your uncle could be responsible for his death?"

"No," he said sharply. "I can't believe Uncle Arthur would do that to my father. I mean, it's his brother, for crying out loud. His flesh and blood. Sorry, I just don't see it."

Sadly, I could. I'd seen relatives, siblings, and spouses all commit the deed before. "He wanted the funeral home badly," I said carefully. "Now he finally has what he wants."

"It has to be someone else." He cursed under his breath. "Now I wish I'd come out last month like I'd planned. See, I was in a wedding for a friend who got married in New York City. I thought about stopping to see my parents for a couple of days, but Mom said it wasn't a good time. I just assumed that they were busy and left it at that."

The piece of paper Charlene mentioned earlier came to mind. "Your father was upset with someone shortly before he died. One of his employees overheard him talking on the phone to someone, asking them how they could do such a thing. Any idea who it might have been?"

"What about the guy who was stealing my father's property? Walt or Wally something. Maybe it was him."

"Sure, that's possible." If we knew what the document was Eddie had been holding, it might lead us to his killer. "What about your father's gambling problem?"

Terry barked out a laugh. "You've got to be kidding me. My father has never had a gambling problem. Jeepers, he found me playing cards with some friends when I was fifteen and grounded me for six months. Dad said it was sinful and I should be ashamed of myself. You must be thinking of someone else."

Okay, this was odd. I tried another direction. "Did your father ever teach you or your mother to do embalming??"

"Yes, I knew how, but I hated it. Just like I hated everything else about the business. As for my mother, no. Dad tried to teach her once, and she passed out. It's not for the faint of heart."

I believed him.

Terry spoke to someone in the background. "Look, I'm sorry, but my wife and I have dinner plans with her boss, and we're already running late. I'll give Mom a call and see if she's got any information that may help."

"That's not necessary—" Before I could say anything further, Terry clicked off.

My father was watching me with a concerned expression on his usually jovial-looking face. "What do you think, baby girl?" he asked.

I handed the phone back to him. "I think I'm confused. Someone's lying, Dad, but who? Did Eddie have a gambling problem or not? If Eddie wasn't stealing from his clients, someone else was doing it. What if he found out and confronted them? Maybe that's why the funeral home was doing poorly." I thought about the document Charlene had seen him holding. "Did Eddie take out a second mortgage on the funeral home?"

Dad shrugged. "I doubt it. He was so proud of the fact that the place was paid off."

Grandma Rosa came into the living room, followed by my mother, who was holding Cookie. "Are you sure about that?" I asked.

"Positive," he said. "Of course, that was his father's doing. It was paid off before he took ownership." He gazed at me thoughtfully. "Seems to me that someone did Eddie wrong, he found out, and they killed him before he could make trouble."

"It's a good theory." I gave Cookie a kiss on the tip of her nose. "I need to leave, but I'll be back in about an hour."

My mother spoke up. "Grandma's going to church, so I'll stay here with Cookie. We'll eat as soon as you both get back."

"Sounds good." Cookie started to giggle, and I remembered Mike's comment how her face lit up whenever she saw me. Her smile was brighter than a ray of sunshine, and it tugged at my heart. Something told me that I shouldn't leave her, but maybe it was just me being overprotective. She was perfectly safe here, and I would be fine too. After all, Josie was coming to meet me.

As I dug my keys out of my purse, I addressed my father. "Do you still happen to have a key to Phibbins?"

He took it off his keyring and handed it to me. "I'm not sure this is still good. Linda said that Arthur was going to change the locks this week."

"Wow, Arthur moves fast."

Grandma Rosa sniffed. "Something is rotten in the state of Denver."

"That's Denmark, Grandma."

She looked puzzled. "Since when is Denmark a state?"

My father snorted. "Something's rotten, for sure. When I talked to Linda on the phone this morning, she said that Arthur was eager to start the transfer. I'm not sure how it could happen so fast, but maybe they'll do it on the honor system for now."

"If the place is free and clear of debt and the will's been read, I'm guessing she could do as she pleases." I shifted from one foot to the other, trying to decide what to do next. If the locks had been changed, was there still a way for me to get in? "Do you think Zach might be there? I need to have a quick talk with him."

My father checked his watch. "It's possible. I mean, the old codger practically lives there." His face suddenly contorted with pain. "Sorry but I think you'll have to go without your old man, baby girl. My Pepto just kicked in."

Ew. "It's okay, Dad."

"Poor sweetie," my mother crooned. "He's been under so much stress lately."

"Let me know what you find out." Dad made a beeline for the stairs. He didn't need to know that I intended to break into Eddie's office if necessary. My father might not appreciate that information.

After giving my baby daughter another kiss, I headed for the front door and felt a hand on my shoulder. My grandmother was standing there watching me, concern etched into her face. The fine wrinkles that surrounded her dark brown eyes were more apparent than usual as she regarded me in silence. She picked up a light sweater and followed me out to the driveway.

"What's wrong?" I asked.

"*Cara mia*, I hope you know what you are doing."

Her perception never ceased to amaze me. "I'm just having a talk with Zach. Besides, Josie will be there. Please don't worry."

"But I always worry. Danger follows you. Keep Josie close."

"I will."

She blew me a kiss as I walked over to my car, parked on the street. Grandma Rosa was still standing beside her Buick in the driveway, her eyes trained on me, as I drove away. For once, I hoped that her instincts would prove wrong.

CHAPTER TWENTY-ONE

––––––

Nagging questions filled my brain as I drove through town to the funeral home. Linda had gone against her husband's wishes and sold the place…to her brother-in-law of all people. Eddie's nemesis. Sure, I understood she needed the money. But it looked like she'd lied about his gambling problem. Was the business really in dire straits? How was I to know for sure?

A tax return from last year or the previous year might help. And there was a good chance I might find them in Eddie's office.

Had Linda done away with Eddie? It didn't seem plausible since she couldn't embalm. She hated everything about the funeral home. The evidence was clearly pointing at Charlene, but it seemed like a convenient setup. Personally, I believed what she'd told Gianna and me. She'd been fond of Eddie and heartbroken by his death. Okay, maybe a bit too fond of him. Then there was Wally, who'd stolen from Eddie and blamed him for his pathetic life. Zach resented Eddie for his demotion, and that left Arthur, who had everything to gain from his brother's death.

The parking lot of Phibbins Mortuary was deserted. I circled the area and then parked my car across the street in front of Starbucks. It would look more conspicuous in an empty lot if say…Arthur happened to drive by or, worse, stop in. I glanced at my watch. Five thirty. Traffic was light for this time of day, but then I remembered it was Good Friday. The Catholic population was high in Colwestern, so a good majority of our townspeople were at church right now, my grandmother included.

I sent Josie a text. *At the funeral home. When will you be here?*

After a couple of minutes, I received a reply. *Sorry. Should be leaving here in about ten minutes. Woman just came in with a huge order, and then I got one for a wedding cake. On my way soon.*

I alighted from the car and crossed the street, making sure to go around to the rear entrance since there was no camera located there. I tapped at the door. No answer. I peered through one of the windows, but the inside was dark. Perfect. Still, I hesitated for a moment. It wasn't really breaking and entering since I had a key, right? This might be my only chance to get inside the building since Arthur was going to change the locks any day. Holding my breath, I inserted the key, and it fit perfectly. For once, things were going as planned, or so I thought.

A loud beeping noise immediately resonated through the walls. Oh crap. I'd forgotten about the alarm!

Frantic, I rushed over to the panel, located on the wall outside of Eddie's office. *What was the code?* My mind was drawing a blank, and I started to panic. Wait a second. My father had been about to tell Brian the code after Eddie's body was discovered. It was his birthday. What was the date? Fourth of July! Good grief, I hoped it didn't include a year. I entered *zero, seven, zero, four*. Nothing. I was running out of time and frantically entered *seven, zero, four*. Thankfully, the beeping stopped immediately. Mentally spent, I exhaled a huge sigh of relief.

I hurried down the hall to the front of the building. I glanced out the window for a full view of the lot, but it was empty. The glass pane in the front door had already been replaced from the firecracker incident. Erring on the side of caution, I checked every room, but no one was in there hiding. When I peeked inside Charlene's work area, I noticed there was a casket with the lid up. A man's body was lying inside. "Excuse me," I whispered and shut the door.

After I'd convinced myself that no one else was here, I opened the door to Eddie's office. There were several cardboard boxes stacked against the wall. It looked like Linda was cleaning out. I sat behind the desk and hesitated. Should I have brought gloves? No, the police had already searched the place, so I should be safe.

The middle drawer was locked, and I cursed under my breath. *All this trouble for nothing.* I checked the drawers on the right-hand side. The top one was also locked, but the bottom drawer, noticeably deeper, slid right open, and then I noticed why. A manila folder was wedged in the side and, as a result, had kept it from closing all the way.

Several other manila folders were lined up in the metal frame, and I let my fingers do the walking through each one. There were invoices, copious notes about what type of services clients wanted for their loved ones, and tax returns. Bingo. The most recent one had been filed in February, two months earlier. I studied the document with interest. I was no accountant, but it was easy to see on the Schedule C that Eddie had made a sizeable profit last year. How interesting. Why had Linda lied?

Another folder contained complaint letters from three families about their loved one's valuables. All of them threatened Phibbins Mortuary with legal action. Eddie had written a letter in return to one family, claiming he had nothing to do with the theft. I wasn't sure if it was a copy from one he'd already mailed or the original. Maybe he'd had second thoughts and decided to let his lawyer handle it. Two of the letters were dated the week before Eddie's death, so it was possible that the families hadn't had a chance to act on them yet.

My cell phone rang at that moment, startling me so badly that I slammed the door shut on my finger. I shook my hand out in pain and withdrew the phone from my jeans pocket. *Gianna.* "Hi. I'm a little busy right now—"

Gianna broke in, her voice quavering with excitement. "Sal, I found out something you'll want to know about in Eddie's will."

"You got a copy?" I asked hopefully.

"Let's just say that Roger Dudley, Eddie's attorney, returned my call after the reading today. He didn't read me the entire document, but he did fill me in on the most important part. You'll never guess who inherited the funeral home."

I stared at the phone, puzzled. "Linda said it was left to her."

"Nope." Gianna sounded pleased with herself. "It went

to Arthur."

I almost fell out of the swivel chair. "But how? Linda said she was one of the witnesses. It was always meant to be hers."

"Well, I don't know what happened, but for some reason, Eddie made a new will the week before he died," Gianna explained. "Roger even admitted to me that he was surprised when Eddie got in touch and demanded it be done right away." She paused. "Roger said he was in such a tizzy about it. Maybe Eddie knew his life was in danger."

The pieces were starting to come together, and I didn't like what they were telling me. "Why would he cut Linda out? Did the document say what would happen to the place once Arthur passed?"

"Roger did share that part with me, but I'm not sure it means anything. If Arthur can't take over or he dies, Phibbins Mortuary would go to Eddie's son, Terry. Linda received nothing. Roger didn't share her reaction, but I suspect she wasn't pleased."

How I would have loved to have been a fly on the wall. "When was the reading?"

"Roger said it was at three o'clock this afternoon."

So Linda had lied. She hadn't gone to New York City. There's no way she would have been back by now. A chill passed over me. She could be on her way to the funeral parlor as we were speaking. I had to get out of here. "This changes everything. Linda's been lying all along."

"But she didn't know until today that she wasn't getting the funeral home," Gianna said. "Unless Eddie told her ahead of time and she became so angry that she killed him."

"She couldn't have killed him. She didn't know the embalming process." Then it hit me. What if Linda had killed him, but someone else had done the dirty work for her?

There was a slight murmur in the background, and then Gianna said, "Tell him I'll be right there. Sal, I have a client waiting for me. I'll call you back in a little while."

She clicked off before I could reply, but it was just as well. I needed to get out of here. It wasn't safe. And where the heck was Josie?

On impulse, I ran my hand around the inside of the drawer casing. An envelope had slid down between the wooden part and the metal file rack. Heart thumping, I opened it and lifted out a document. The paper was for dissolution of marriage by one Edward Phibbins. My jaw dropped. I hadn't been expecting this. Eddie had been planning to divorce Linda. The document's date was the day before he'd disappeared. Linda had not signed the form, so perhaps she had never been served. Still, she must have known.

Charlene had overheard Eddie on the phone, crying, *How could you do this to me?* Had Linda been the one ripping off Eddie's clientele? That would have been too much for honest Eddie to take, so he may have decided to file for divorce. Linda may have planned to do away with him before he got the chance and sell the funeral home to make a profit. But karma had intervened. It might be too late for Eddie, but at least he'd gotten the last word.

I snapped a picture of the document with my phone, returned it to the desk, and closed the drawer. Josie should have been here be now, and the clock was ticking away precious minutes for me. I needed to call Brian, but it would have to wait until I was safe in my car. After switching off the light, I backed out of the office and shut the door.

I turned around to find Linda watching me, an evil smile spreading across her face.

"Hello, Sally," she greeted me. "I hope you found everything you were looking for?"

My blood turned to ice when I looked into her eyes. Like a river running through the night, they were endless, dark, and cold.

I struggled to compose myself. "Oh, hi, Linda. I'm glad you're here. The back door was unlocked, so I decided to come in and wait for you. I have news that I wanted to share."

She drew her eyebrows together. "What news? I haven't heard of anything."

Stay calm, Sal. Linda didn't appear to be armed and had at least thirty years on me. I could manage to get away from her. My phone beeped, but I didn't dare pull it out. Josie had most likely arrived and was in the lot, so I tried not to panic. "Yes.

News about Charlene. You know that she's been arrested, right?"

She snickered. "Please. That's old news. Everyone already knows. And the back door wasn't unlocked. Why don't you come clean? I know exactly what you've been up to."

I took a step in the direction of the back door. "What do you mean?"

Linda looked at me like I was a moron. "My son just called me and said that you and your dopey father have been harassing him. The camera outside is viewable from my computer at home. I saw you crossing the street from Starbucks." Her eyes glittered with anger. "Hope your last latte tasted delicious."

She grabbed my arm in a death-like grip, and I yelped. "Let go of me!"

Linda produced a pocketknife from her jacket and raised it in the air. Fear lodged in my throat. My body went numb as she pressed me up against the wall.

"You wouldn't use that," I whispered.

She narrowed her eyes. "I don't want to, but I'll do what I have to. You're not giving me much choice. Stupid me. When your idiot father suggested you come here with the cookies, I thought, it's a good cover-up. No one will think I have anything to hide if I let the dynamic duo from Sally's Samples in here. I figured, how much of a pain can she really be? Not as bad as her father, that's for sure. But I was wrong. You're ten times worse. Like a dog with a bone. You can't let anything go."

I tried to stall for time. What the heck was Josie doing? Baking a cake? "You were stealing the jewelry from clients to support your gambling habit. Eddie found out and decided to divorce you, didn't he?"

She looked at me, visibly impressed. "Well, I was wrong. You're not as stupid as your father. Yeah, Eddie gave me no choice. That was the one thing he could never tolerate—abuse of his clients and the business. If I'd had an affair, he would have been more forgiving. Eddie lived and died for this place." She gave a harsh laugh. "Yes, pun intended."

Bile rose in the back of my throat. "You're sick."

"Not really," she said. "I just need to protect my interests. Eddie got in the way, and now you're doing the same thing. Believe me, getting rid of you will weigh a lot less on my conscience than Eddie's death."

The sound of tires crunching on the pavement met our ears. Thank God for Josie. Linda cocked her head in the direction of the parking lot, and I took that split second to shove her backwards. She hit her head against the wall, and the knife fell to the floor. There was no time to pick it up. I turned on my heel and fled for the back door.

A car door slammed, and relief soared through me. Josie to the rescue. Everything would be okay now.

Linda screamed at me to stop, but I'd gotten a good head start. I threw the door open and glanced around, searching for Josie's minivan. "Help!" I screamed. "This woman's a killer!"

A man was standing on the small back porch, blocking my path to the lot. I tried to stop and turn around, but it was too late. He reached forward and grabbed me. I struggled, lost my balance, and fell down the stairs. My head hit the cement, and I landed in a heap on the pavement.

"Get her back inside before someone sees!" Linda panted from the doorway.

I tried to stand, but the man quickly half dragged, half carried me up the three steps back inside. My head throbbed painfully as I kicked and fought. I was dumped on the floor and heard the back door click behind me. I reached up and clawed at Linda's leg with my nails, and she returned the favor by kicking me in the side. The pain was blinding, and I struggled to keep from blacking out. Defeated, I finally lay still on my stomach.

There had been no Josie waiting outside. Whenever she did arrive, it would be too late for me. I'd chosen the wrong exit to seek my escape. The story of my life.

"Good thing you got here when you did." Linda was breathing hard. "That little snit would have gotten away, and we can't have that. She knows too much."

"No worries," came a deep, throaty laugh. "We can handle her."

My earlier suspicions were confirmed. The man dragged me up the hall toward the display room. My face burned painfully from contact with the rug, and the pain in my side was so bad that I wondered if I'd broken a rib. I started to scream.

"Shut up!" Linda yelled and shoved a rolled-up cloth in my mouth.

Cold, stark fear consumed my body. Rough hands flipped me onto my back. I blinked and looked up. The picture before me was fuzzy, but I could see the cruel, triumphant-like smile on Linda's face. Standing next to her was Arthur. I'd guessed he was involved but unfortunately, it had taken me a little too long to figure it all out. I'd dismissed Linda from killing Eddie by herself because of the after-death process that had to be followed. That's where Arthur and his funeral home training had come in.

It was as if he'd guessed what I'd been thinking. "No time to embalm Betty Crocker. People will be looking for her soon. She's got a baby, right? We'll just have to dispose of her."

"Someone must know she's here," Linda said in a concerned voice.

Arthur laughed. "No worries. Charlene's out on bail today, and I can make it look like she came here to meet Nancy Drew. They argued, and *poof!* Charlene killed her. As usual, I'll organize everything. I'm good at it, remember? A hell of a lot better than you."

He learned over me as I managed to draw my leg up, and my foot connected with his prized male organs. He let out a yelp, groaned, and stumbled backwards. I got to my feet shakily.

"Do something!" he screamed at Linda. "Don't just stand there!"

Linda lunged forward with her bony fingers and grabbed my neck in a choke hold. She started to apply pressure, and it was only seconds before I was losing consciousness.

"You did this to yourself," she hissed into my ear.

My last thought before passing out was to wonder what my precious baby would do without me.

CHAPTER TWENTY-TWO

———

My eyelids were heavy when I opened them to complete blackness. Where was I? How had it gotten so dark already? I blinked a few times, but the blackness didn't disappear. The air was warm and confined, triggering a clammy sensation in me. My brain was foggy as I tried to recall what had happened. The last thing I remembered was Linda's hands around my neck. My head ached, and my throat was parched. I had no idea where I was, but at least I was alive. Blissfully alive.

Sweat trickled down my face as I tried to raise my head, but it connected with something solid, forcing me down on my back. There was movement underneath me, and I knew I was in some type of vehicle. Why couldn't I see anything? A horn blared in the distance. Where were we going? Was I in the trunk?

Terror seized me, and I wondered what they planned to do with me. I reached my hands out on either side, hoping there might be a tool in the trunk I could use. My arms couldn't stretch out completely. There was some type of wall on each side of me. I put my palms above my head, and there was one there too. Whatever I was in began to rock slightly from side to side. A box of some sort. *Oh God.* A terrifying realization occurred to me.

I'm inside a coffin. They're going to bury me, like they had planned for Eddie.

I took several deep breaths, trying hard not to hyperventilate and remain focused. Now was not the time to panic. *Think, Sal. Think.*

Tears streamed down my face. I'd always been claustrophobic and not a fan of the dark. Mike had often teased me that the nightlight in Cookie's room was more for my benefit than hers. How much air was left in this thing? Could anyone outside hear me if I screamed?

The vehicle stopped, but before I could open my mouth, loud angry voices commenced from behind me.

"You stupid idiot," Arthur growled. "How the hell did I let you drag me into this?"

"It's too late now," Linda retorted. "And you'd better make sure I get the twenty grand that you promised me."

Arthur cackled like a witch. "Why should I give you anything? Boy, you played me like a violin. Got me to do all your dirty work for you. If I'd known that Eddie changed the will, I never would have helped you do away with him."

"You wanted him gone too," she shot back.

"Yes, but I didn't know you'd already offed him," he retorted angrily. "I told you to wait, but no, you wouldn't listen. He told me on the phone that he wanted to make amends—that it had been too long. Then he said he wanted to talk to me about something else. Probably where to find a good divorce lawyer."

She laughed. "You're crazy."

"I could have worked things out with him. If I'd have known he was leaving me the funeral home in his will, I never would have helped you. But he was already dead when I got there. What a fool I was. I should have run away and let you embalm and bury him yourself."

"Shut up! I still can't believe he'd disinherit me like that."

He grunted. "Then you're dumber than I thought. What I don't understood is that after you begged me to help dispose of him, you up and leave his body there? You were supposed to stay with him at the funeral home until I got back. What the hell were you thinking?"

"It was only for an hour." Linda's tone became defensive. "How was I supposed to know that moron friend of his would turn up looking to take a nap? Dom Muccio is a wacko. I had no idea Eddie had given him a key."

The car jerked forward again, and I assumed that the light must have changed. They continued squabbling, but it was difficult to hear everything over the sound of the vehicle. Most of my questions had already been answered. Linda had killed

Eddie with the cyanide. She and Arthur had previously discussed killing him. Perhaps she was going to stage it to look like someone else had committed the murder. I wasn't sure. Arthur had turned up to meet with Eddie but instead found Linda with a dead body. They'd put aside their animosity to dispose of Eddie. They weren't having an affair either—at least that was one thing they hadn't pretended about. It was obvious they couldn't stand each other.

The car stopped again, and Linda's words floated through the air. "If I'd known he was going to change the will and leave the funeral parlor to you, I never would have killed him. What would have been the point? So you owe me. I don't care what the will says. Part of the place belongs to me, so you'd better pay up."

I brought my hand to my mouth in horror. Poor Eddie's death could have easily been avoided, but Linda's greed had instigated his killing. His own wife! She'd been sure she'd inherit the funeral home then sell it to Arthur for a nice profit. She'd played the brokenhearted widow to a tee, sobbing her heart out, not wanting to sell but being forced to for need of the income. It had all been a lie.

Arthur, in turn, thought he would profit by Linda selling the funeral home to him at a cheaper price, which was why he'd helped her prepare Eddie for burial. He hadn't known the funeral home had been left to him. Yes, Karma had come to call, but not soon enough to save Eddie.

The vehicle was still moving. With terror I realized I was taking the ride that had been meant for Eddie. Were we going to a cemetery? Tears began to flow down my cheeks. I closed my eyes against the darkness and tried to concentrate. After all the near-death experiences I'd been through before, this might be the most terrifying.

I reached above my head and pushed hard on the lid, but it didn't budge. Was I in a pine box like Eddie? They wouldn't throw good money away on the likes of me. My father had told me about the cheap clasp on the outside. I pushed harder, but the lid refused to budge.

Arthur grunted loudly from behind me, startling me out of my thoughts. "I know you were angry about the will, but damn it, woman. You almost gave yourself away when Dom stopped by with his daughter. Your ranting about how nothing was fair was a bit over the top, even for you."

"I was upset," she admitted. "How did you want me to act? They seemed to buy it."

"No, they didn't!" he roared. "Maybe he did, but I could tell by the look on his daughter's face that she didn't believe it. She was suspicious of us from the beginning."

Yes, my face was literally going to be the death of me.

"You weren't much better. Wanting to hire his stupid blog service? Then going to see her about the coffin cookies?" Linda asked in disbelief.

The car started again. "Hey, that blog is genius. It would be good advertising for the place. Dom's ego is a mile long, so I was just feeding it. Besides, I knew she'd say no about the cookies. That was just a cover-up. She's been suspicious of me since I walked in on you two in Eddie's office."

"You wanted them to suspect me all along. Have them think that I did it. You never could be trusted," she said angrily.

"And you could?" he laughed. "You wanted everyone to think I killed Eddie. I know you were saying stuff behind my back. The day he died, he told me on the phone about your little gambling debt. You disgusted him. Why he didn't divorce you sooner, I'll never know. Hell, I'm not sure why he ever married you. Plenty of other fish in the sea and better looking as well."

The car swerved, and Linda shouted something. It was getting more difficult to breathe inside the coffin. If they were fighting, we might get into an accident, but that wasn't necessarily a bad thing. It could bring the police, who I sorely needed right now.

The coffin shifted and moved against one side of the vehicle. In desperation, I pushed on the lid again. Sweat and tears mixed together and ran down my face, and it was becoming more difficult to remain calm. This time I heard a satisfying click, and the lid moved slightly. Thank God. I inhaled several gulps of air then was forced to put the lid back in place. It was too heavy to hold up for long and I didn't want to take a chance that Linda or Arthur might see any movement.

The vehicle slowed, and we started going uphill. We

must be near our destination. I had no idea how long I'd been unconscious after Linda had choked me. I lifted the lid again. Whatever sunlight was left was quickly evaporating, so chances were that it had to be after seven o'clock. Someway, somehow, I'd have to surprise Linda and Arthur when they lifted the coffin out of the vehicle. But there were two of them and only one of me. The odds weren't in my favor, so how was I going to pull this off?

I simply had no choice. I needed to live—for my baby, for Mike, for my family. Mike always joked that I had nine lives like a cat. I prayed that I hadn't used up all of them.

My family had to be worried, and Josie must be going crazy by now. Grandma Rosa had been wary before she left for church. A sickening thought swept through me. What if Josie had arrived before Linda and Arthur had left? Did they attack her too?

For the moment, I had to concentrate all my efforts on getting myself out of here. When Josie arrived at the funeral home, she would have immediately sensed something was wrong and alerted the police. Would they know to look for me in a graveyard?

I felt inside my jean pockets. My cell phone was gone, as I'd suspected. The pictures I'd taken of the divorce document were on it, but Linda and Arthur had probably already disposed of them. The vehicle was moving more slowly, and I tried to prepare myself. It would stop soon, and then they would be coming for me. If only there was some way that I could defend myself. I felt around in the darkness but knew there was nothing inside the coffin except for me. There might be something in the back of the hearse I could use as a weapon, but it would be too risky to climb out and look.

I ran my hands over my shirt and jeans and connected with something in the pocket. Confused, I pulled it out. My fingers wrapped around a plastic object and a soft piece of cloth. My heart instantly melted. Cookie's new rattle.

The vehicle stopped, and a car door slammed. My heart thumped loudly against the wall of my chest. This was it. They were coming.

"Get your lazy behind out here and help me," Arthur

yelled.

"Forget it," Linda shouted back. "You can lift her by yourself. The grave's already dug. It's for the Morgan funeral tomorrow. I'll send the guys a text later to dig a fresh one—say that I forgot about a body or something."

Arthur muttered, "I hate that you've gotten me into this. We need to move fast."

"They can't prove anything." Linda sounded bored, like she had better things to do. "No body, no evidence. That's the way it works, brother dear. I hope she can hear me if she didn't already die of fright. Betty Crocker deserves it for all her snooping. She should have minded her own business."

"You're one crazy broad." Arthur said something else in an undertone, but I couldn't make it out. "How the hell am I going to lift her all by myself?"

"Eddie said you once bench-pressed 250 pounds," Linda yelled. "She can't weigh that much."

There was a thud, which must have been the back door of the hearse opening. Suddenly, the coffin and me were sliding across the back of the vehicle.

Arthur muttered something about "heavier than she looks." The coffin crashed to the ground and wobbled for a few seconds. He yelled again for Linda. "Get over here now and help me. I can't move this thing alone!"

It was the split second I was waiting for. I threw open the lid, pressed the button on Cookie's rattle, and shone the light into Arthur's surprised face.

He blinked and shielded his eyes while I jumped out of the coffin. My foot connected with the wood, and I stumbled to the ground. I was surprised at how weak I felt, but I had more important things to think about—my life, for one. I started to scream for help at the top of my lungs as I ran down a neat row of cemetery plots and one freshly dug grave. Was that the one meant for me?

"Get back here!" Arthur shouted and then proceeded to call me every vile name he could think of.

Footsteps pounded the ground behind me. Darkness had started to descend, and I glanced around the cemetery, unsure of which way to go. There wasn't a living soul in sight. Okay, people didn't often visit cemeteries at night, but I could have used any help I could come by. I ran on, still unsure of where I was headed.

We were in Colwestern's cemetery, but I wasn't very familiar with the place. My grandfather was buried here, but I hadn't been out to visit him for a couple of years. Grandma Rosa came faithfully once a week. How I wished I'd come last month when she'd asked me, but it had been after one of Cookie's sleepless nights. Now I was paying the price for being an awful granddaughter.

Thankfully, there was a full moon, which helped to guide me. A bout of nausea almost brought me to my knees, but I forced myself to go on. I had no idea where this would lead, and tried to keep my eyes peeled for a wrought iron gate that meant I was at the cemetery's entrance. My vision blurred from dizziness, causing me to stumble, and I almost ran straight into a tree.

The blessed sound of a siren wailed in the distance. It grew closer, but I couldn't stop yet. Was someone coming for me? I couldn't stop to find out. My lungs were ready to burst. At that moment, the front gate came into view. I ran toward it as a yell sounded from behind. Arthur tackled me to the ground like a football player.

The blow stunned me and had affected Arthur as well. He was breathing heavily as he landed on top of me. I managed to roll to my side and lifted my leg, which connected with his stomach. He staggered for a second then came at me again, this time smacking me hard across the face. He pinned one of my arms with his hand while I struggled.

"Let go of me!" I screamed.

"You're not going to ruin everything!" Arthur shrieked. The moon reflected off his face. His hair was disheveled, streaks of dirt ran down his cheeks, and spit had collected at the corners of his mouth. He reached for my neck, as if to trying to force me into unconsciousness again, but I grabbed his hand and bit it as hard as I could. He let out a bloodcurdling scream. There was a shovel lying a few feet away. My fingers connected with the handle as Arthur clamped a hand over my mouth and nose. I struggled under the pressure but managed to lift the shovel and brought it down on the side of his head. For a few seconds, Arthur remained motionless above me, staring into my eyes. Then he fell forward, collapsing onto my chest.

Breathing heavily, I managed to roll Arthur off me and stagger to my feet, but my victory was short lived. Someone pushed me from behind, and I fell to the ground. Linda stood over me, her evil smile in place once again. I raised an arm above my head in a vain attempt to protect myself.

Linda laughed as she picked up the shovel. "Say good night, Sally."

"Hold it right there!" Brian called. We turned our heads, and I could see the shadows of two figures nearby. Both came into closer view. Adam was with him, and they both had their guns trained on Linda. She clutched the shovel between her hands, stared at them and then back at me.

Brian clicked the safety on his gun. "I wouldn't if I were you."

Linda let the shovel slide to the ground, inches away from my head. Adam sprang forward and drew a pair of handcuffs from his belt, placing them around Linda's wrists. "Linda Phibbins, you're under arrest for the murder of Eddie Phibbins and the kidnapping of Sally Donovan. You have the right to remain silent…"

Linda started sobbing as Adam led her away to the squad car. Another siren screamed in the distance as Brian rushed forward and helped me to my feet. Another officer appeared and, after conferring with Brian, placed handcuffs on Arthur, still motionless on the ground.

I leaned against Brian for support. "Thanks for getting here in the nick of time."

He shot me a worried glance. "You look terrible and definitely in need of medical attention. There's a huge lump on your head."

"Nothing new, right?"

Brian almost smiled as he put a hand on my elbow and led me to an EMT vehicle that had just pulled up. His expression was grim. "Did they have you tied up in the hearse?"

"No." My voice cracked. "I was in a coffin. They were going to bury me alive."

Brian sucked in some air. "Sally, it may be time to hang up your sleuthing apron. I thought having a gun to your head was the worst thing that could happen to you, but apparently I was wrong."

The EMT led me to the back of the vehicle, where he examined my head.

"I thought so too, but I'm here to tell the tale, and Eddie's gotten justice. Maybe something good will come out of this."

"Like what?" Brian asked.

Josie's minivan screeched to a stop next to the cruiser. As she ran over to us, I gave Brian a weak smile. "No idea. It's just a feeling I have."

CHAPTER TWENTY-THREE

After I'd been checked over, Brian insisted on driving me to the hospital for further tests. Josie followed us in her van and then sat with me in one of the curtained-off areas of the emergency room after I'd been examined.

"There's no need for you to stay," I assured her. "Rob's waiting for you, and Mike's on his way." Josie had called him since my phone was nowhere to be found, but that was the least of my worries.

She waved a hand. "It's not a big deal."

"But we've got all those orders for tomorrow," I protested. "It's the day before Easter, and we've got our work cut out for us. You said you'd be at the bakery at five o'clock, so go home and get some sleep."

Josie checked her watch and blew out a sigh. "Sal, I couldn't care less about that. This is all my fault. I should have realized how dire the situation was. If I'd gotten to the funeral parlor sooner, none of this would have happened."

"It's not your fault. You called Brian and alerted him where to look for me."

She clenched her fists at her sides. "When I saw your car at Starbucks and that the lights were off in Phibbins, I knew something was wrong. I probably just missed Arthur and Linda taking off with you. I noticed the hearse was missing and thought the worst. I ran back to Starbucks and searched every inch of the place. You have no idea how freaked out I was. I should never have let you go alone."

"There wasn't any way to know what would happen," I said. "Linda lied about being out of town, so I thought we'd be safe to snoop around. Please stop beating yourself up over this.

Thanks to you, the police arrived in the nick of time. Now go home. You need your rest. Tomorrow's one of our busiest days of the year, and Dodie can't handle it alone."

She stared at me curiously. "You're not thinking about coming in tomorrow, are you?"

"If they let me go home and the doctor gives me a clean bill of health, I'll be there. But not at five o'clock," I teased.

Josie didn't laugh. "No, Sal. You should take it easy tomorrow. Stay home and rest. You've been through quite an ordeal."

"I'm here, and I'm alive. I've got a slightly bruised rib, but he's taped me up, and I'm okay. If possible, I'll be there. Now humor me, and go home. Please?"

Josie's eyes started to mist over and looking into those large blue pools that resembled the ocean made me want to weep as well. She leaned in and hugged me tightly. "Love you, partner. There's nothing I wouldn't do for you."

"Same here," I said hoarsely.

Josie moved aside the curtain. "Text me when you're home, okay?" She waved, and then disappeared. I heard her speaking to someone on the other side, and a couple of seconds later Brian poked his head in.

"Okay to come in?"

"Of course." I smiled. "I thought maybe you'd left."

He shook his head. "Nope. I wanted to make sure you were okay before I went back to work. Josie said you had a slight concussion and a bruised rib. Is Mike on his way?"

"Yes, she called him for me. He was working out of town today but should be here soon."

He sat down next to me. "You're lucky the fright alone didn't kill you. Other people might not have fared as well, Sally. All these brushes with murder have made you tough."

"Let's not talk about it anymore," I suggested. "There's more pleasant things for me to think about, like my daughter."

"Sounds like a good plan," he agreed.

"What's going on with our friendly funeral owners? I was able to overhear enough of Linda and Arthur's conversation to know that they were both responsible for Eddie's death, although Linda was the one who actually poisoned him."

Brian's smile disappeared. "Those two are quite a pair. Adam said they kept shouting in the cruiser, saying that the other one was responsible for Eddie's death. Linda did make a full confession a short time ago. Then she told Adam that it was all Eddie's fault for changing the will without telling her." He shook his head in disbelief.

"Linda also made up the story about Eddie having a gambling problem in order to cover that she was the one with the addiction. I'm certain she was selling off the deceased's personal items, but don't know if she confessed to that. It's amazing how they were married for so long and that he never really knew her."

Brian twisted his gold wedding band around his finger. "I haven't had a chance to tell you yet, but we do have proof. Adam and I have been going around to pawnshops with her, Arthur's, and Charlene's pictures. One owner identified Linda earlier, saying that she came in with a diamond ring just yesterday. Turns out it belonged to Evelyn Peacock, whose service was at Phibbins the other day. The ring returned to her husband was a fake. Too bad for Linda that she didn't know when to quit."

"Gamblers are like that," I said. "As far as I'm concerned, Arthur is just as bad as his sister-in-law. He was planning to kill Eddie, but Linda went ahead without him. Neither one will make bail, will they?"

Brian shook his head. "He may not have been the one to actually poison Arthur, but he was an accomplice. Plus, he kidnapped you. No, I think it's safe to say they won't be bothering you for a long time."

I pressed my hands against my side which was throbbing a bit. "Linda used cyanide on him but I don't know how."

"She fixed him a cup of tea when they were alone in the funeral home. Eddie died within minutes. Apparently, Linda hadn't thought the scheme out all the way and was struggling to get him into the coffin when Arthur showed up. Eddie had called him earlier to come over, most likely to discuss the change in his will."

"It's so awful," I said sadly.

Brian's mouth formed a thin, hard line. "Linda had promised Arthur she'd sell him the funeral home cheap. But when they found out that Eddie had changed his will, Arthur wanted her to disappear forever, so he agreed to give her money if she left town. There was an airline ticket to Mexico in Linda's purse for a ten o'clock flight tonight."

"Then she lied about going to live with her son?" I asked.

"Looks like," he answered. "Terry knew nothing about it. We have no reason to believe he was involved with the scheme to kill his father."

Jeez, had Linda told the truth about anything? "What's happening with Charlene?"

"She's been released," Brian said. "She said she wants to forget about this nightmare. Charlene doesn't care who ends up with the funeral parlor. There's no way she'll ever go back there."

"I can't say I blame her."

The blue curtain rustled, and Mike peered in. Our eyes met, and he was at my side in a second. Brian stood and stepped aside as Mike's arms went around me. He drew back and pushed my hair away from my face. "Princess, are you okay?"

"Yes, now that you're here." I leaned up to kiss him.

Mike cupped my face between his hands. "You gave me such a scare. You have to stop doing that."

"She's good at it," Brian agreed, then his face instantly reddened. "Um, I need to get back to work, so I'll leave you two alone."

Mike stretched out his hand to him. "Thanks so much for taking care of her. I appreciate it."

"No need to thank me." Brian looked amused. "She took care of this one by herself. She's pretty good with a shovel. Hey, Sally, if you ever want a job at the police department, I think we can hook you up."

I buried my face in Mike's neck. "I'll keep it in mind, thanks. Tell Ally I said hello."

"Will do, but she's not working tonight. She's at a bachelorette party for a friend who's getting married." He grinned at us. "I think we started something. We've got two weddings to attend next month and another one in June."

"Well, remember where to send them for cookies. Josie makes wedding cakes too." I couldn't resist going a little further.

"And she's created some terrific cakes for baby showers."

Brian smiled. "We may be taking you up on that soon. Okay, you guys take care of yourselves and enjoy the holiday tomorrow. Until next time, Sally."

I shuddered. "I hope there isn't a next time."

"You and me both," he said. "But this is *you* we're talking about." He moved the curtain aside and disappeared.

Mike blew out a sigh. "I wish he hadn't said that. I always hope you're done finding dead bodies."

"I didn't find Eddie. My father did."

He ran an agitated hand through his hair. "Well, at least your morbid father is done with Phibbins forever."

I loved the feel of his strong, protective arms around me. "I wonder what's going to happen to it now."

Before Mike could respond, a nurse came into the room. She smiled at Mike and then addressed me. "The doctor said you can go home, Mrs. Donovan. He has a few instructions for you to follow. I'll be back with them in a second."

"Thank you." I stood, and Mike handed me my purse. "I'm starved. I hope Grandma saved us some lasagna."

Mike pressed his lips into my hair. "Since we have to stop and pick up Cookie anyway, I'm sure your grandmother won't let us leave until we've been well fed." He paused. "Sal, I know you tried to stay out of this and am sorry for the way I acted."

I stared up into his handsome and concerned face. "After the fire at Nicoletta's house, it became obvious that my family might be in danger. I couldn't walk away then."

"I know that, princess." His eyes stared soberly into mine. "But I can't stop thinking about how terrified you must have felt in that coffin. I can't even begin to imagine what that was like for you, and I don't want to."

"Let's change the subject." For a brief moment, I let myself reflect on the other ordeals I'd been through, which consisted of being threatened with a gun, tied up and left to die in an apartment filled with natural gas, and locked in a freezer alongside a killer. They had all been horrible experiences, but each incident had made me stronger. Somehow, I would move on from this, go back to work tomorrow, and bask in the love of my husband, daughter, and family—until it happened again. Or would it? There was no way to know for certain.

Until then, all I could do was live my life with love, laughter, and happiness. With a little bit of luck, I'd persevere for a long time to come. My grandmother had once told me that I may have been put on this earth for the sole reason to help people. It was an awesome responsibility and a bit scary at times.

I snuggled closer to my husband. "As long as I have you and Cookie, I'll always be fine."

"I owe you another apology." Mike's lips were beside my ear.

"For what?"

Mike caressed my cheek with his finger. "I guess I've been feeling kind of neglected lately. It's silly, I know. With our hectic work schedules and the baby, we never have time for each other. I think that's important for a marriage. We should definitely do date nights once in a while, but I was thinking more about myself than you. The bakery, taking care of Cookie, and your father asking for help. It's a lot for anyone to deal with. I should have been more understanding."

"You have a lot on your plate too."

He leaned in to kiss me. "Yes, but if you'd turned down your father—well, that wouldn't have been you being you."

I smiled. "He really didn't give me much choice."

"That's not the point." His expression turned serious. "I don't want you to think I'm not supportive. Even though I may hate the dangerous situations you've been involved in, I'll always be there for you. I never want to let you down."

"You won't," I insisted. "The past few months have been a big adjustment for both of us since we became parents. It's been wonderful, and I'm so thankful for our little girl. But it's also been tougher than I ever imagined. I look at people like Josie and am amazed at how she manages to do all that she does. I appreciate her even more now."

"We simply have to work at making more time for ourselves. Especially if we plan to add on to our family." Mike winked.

"I want that more than anything," I said softly. "This experience with Eddie and his family has taught me how lucky I am to have mine. All I want is to continue running my bakery with my best friend, be a good mom to Cookie, and have you by my side."

He put an arm around my waist. "Come on. Let's go find the nurse and get out of here. Cookie's waiting to see her mommy and looking forward to her first Easter Sunday, with a big chocolate bunny to boot."

"She can't have chocolate yet," I laughed. "Besides, she doesn't have any teeth."

His eyes twinkled into mine. "I guess we'll have to take care of it for her, then. Sunday is a day to rejoice and be thankful. And I have a lot to be thankful for."

"We both do," I said as he kissed me again.

CHAPTER TWENTY-FOUR

———

"Look at this, baby girl," my father called over to me. "Cookie's got quite the grip on her. We might make a baseball player out of her yet."

Gianna frowned at my father from her place on the living room floor. Next to her was Alex, who was holding a chocolate bunny in one hand and a toy basketball in the other. My father was on the couch next to my mother, with Cookie on her lap. Cookie had grabbed hold of my father's finger and was squealing in delight as he made comical faces at her. Johnny was seated in the dining room, talking quietly to his grandmother, while I helped Grandma Rosa set the table for an early dinner.

Cookie's Easter basket was next to Alex's but filled with slightly different things. There was the traditional chocolate bunny I'd always received as a child, about a foot tall. I had no idea what we were going to do with it. There was also a sippy cup, more rattles, a new dress, and the books *Pat the Bunny* and *Peter Rabbit*. My little girl looked adorable in a floral white and pink dress, matching pink jacket, and bonnet. She also had on white tights and black patent leather shoes that complemented the outfit.

We were all dressed in our Sunday finest and had just returned from morning mass. The church had been packed with standing room only, and we'd stayed for the Easter egg hunt afterwards. Although Cookie wasn't old enough to participate, Mike had carried her around the yard and picked out a couple of decorated eggs for her. Next year she would be walking on her own for the egg hunt, and I couldn't wait to see her in action.

Mike and I hadn't attended church in over a year, and I planned to remedy that. I'd been dreadful about it ever since I left home to marry Colin. My parents and grandmother went faithfully every week. Mike had only been a handful of times during his life, but when I'd asked him about going today, he'd been surprisingly receptive. We'd even chatted with the priest about having Cookie baptized.

While the others relaxed in the living room, I went back into the kitchen to see what else I could do to assist Grandma Rosa. She waved me away. "You go and enjoy yourself, *cara mia*. You have been through a lot this week and deserve some up time."

"I think you mean downtime," I suggested.

She nodded. "I like that too."

My stomach growled as I helped her arrange the dishes on the dining room table. There was baked ham with cloves and her fabulous brown sugar glaze, but my favorite traditional Italian dishes were there as well, including braciole, pasta, and stuffed peppers. There were also mashed potatoes, antipasto, and a variety of desserts, such as tiramisu and cheesecake. I worried that if we didn't eat soon, I might start drooling.

"Everything smells wonderful," I told her, but this was no surprise. My grandmother's food was always perfection. She cooked from the heart, which was why it seemed like she did it all with minimal effort. Even though she was in her late seventies, she showed no sign of slowing down, for which I was eternally grateful. She was the glue that held our family together or, more appropriately, the ricotta of our cheesecake.

Grandma Rosa and I returned to the kitchen, where I filled a carafe with coffee. "We take you for granted," I told her.

"Bah." She walked back into the dining room, and I followed. "I enjoy doing this. And it makes my heart sing to see the little ones. I hope that there will be many more."

"We're working on it," Mike teased as he came up behind me and put his arms around my waist. "Rosa, why don't you let me carry the ham in?"

She accepted his offer. After Mike went into the kitchen, she smiled fondly at me and set a bottle of red wine on the table next to her rose-patterned china. "Things are better between you two now, yes?"

I stared at her in amazement. "How did you know?"

"I know everything," Grandma Rosa said. "No, I am only kidding. But it has been easy to see how tired you both are, *cara mia*. It is not easy to have a baby and try to make time for each other, plus your jobs. You must work at it." She tapped the bottle. "A good marriage—what is the saying? It is like a fine wine. It only gets better with age."

"Did someone say wine?" Gianna asked as she came into the room. She grabbed a glass and filled it with merlot. "Don't mind if I do." She put an arm around my shoulders and studied the bump on my forehead. "I can't believe you worked a full day yesterday," she scolded. "I told you I would have come in to help."

"I wanted to do it. Besides, you have enough going on in your own life." I'd even brought Cookie in for a couple of hours, but my mother had come to get her after her hair appointment.

Since my latest brush with death, I was looking at life through fresh, new eyes. Cookie had woken up twice last night, but instead of trying to pretend I was asleep, I'd gone right in to her, despite Mike offering. Sure, I was tired today, but I was more determined than ever to treasure those tender moments with my daughter—even at three o'clock in the morning. Things could have ended much differently the other day, and I was thankful to still be here.

Gianna took a sip of the wine and pursed her lips. "I spoke to Roger this morning. He couldn't believe it when he heard about Linda. He's known Eddie for years and always thought they had a solid marriage. Roger said he never thought she was capable of such a thing."

"Addiction changes people. Then again, maybe she was always devious like that. We'll never know for sure," I said. "Did Roger say what's happening with the funeral parlor?"

Gianna shook her head. "He mentioned that Terry was flying out here in a couple of days. Since Terry hates the business, Roger's guessing he'll sell."

"Yeah, it was pretty obvious that he wasn't interested when I spoke to him." My heart went out to Eddie. At least he'd gotten justice, but he'd been horribly deceived by two people he thought he could trust. It was a sad ending for Phibbins Mortuary.

"Come along now," Grandma Rosa said. "Everything is ready."

Gianna, Mike, and I started to help ourselves. I then took Cookie from my father and placed her in the bouncy seat next to me while Gianna strapped Alex into his high chair between herself and Johnny. We all chatted as we passed the dishes, laughing and in good spirits. I made sure to take a little of everything. Food tasted better than before. It was funny how I always appreciated the simple things in life more after mine had been threatened.

Mike spooned cereal into Cookie's eager mouth from a bowl that Grandma Rosa had brought him. He smiled tenderly at me as I placed ham, mashed potatoes, and stuffed peppers on his plate. "All my favorites. You know just what I like, princess."

Heat rose in my cheeks. Of course, he was referring to something else—the intimate moments we'd shared last night before Cookie had woken up. Things wouldn't change for a while, and we wouldn't have much time alone, but that was okay. We loved and appreciated each other, and it was more than enough.

My mother handed an envelope to me and one to Gianna. "This is just a little something from your father and me for our wonderful daughters, who have given us such beautiful grandchildren." She beamed at my father, but he was already involved in an intimate relationship with his braciole.

"Whatever you say, hot stuff," he said absently.

"You didn't have to do anything." My jaw dropped when I saw what was inside. It was a certificate for dinner and an overnight stay at the Wallingford Hotel, an elite hotel and spa just outside of Colwestern. "Mom, Dad, this is fabulous!"

Mom looked pleased with herself. "Your stay is for next Saturday night, Sal, and Gianna's the following weekend. Of course, we'll watch the babies while you lovebirds go off and enjoy yourselves. We thought you both needed a little getaway, especially with everything that's happened lately."

Gianna looked misty-eyed and was speechless for a moment. She slid back her chair and went around the table to give our mother and father each a kiss. I did the same. "Thank you so much," she said. "This is very thoughtful."

"It really is, Maria and Dom," Mike said as he wiped Cookie's mouth.

Johnny grinned and raised a glass to them. "This is great. Thanks a million."

My father squeezed my mother's hand. "Aw, shucks. We're happy to do it."

Mom beamed. "Well, I'll be honest, girls. It's just part of my scheme to get more grandchildren."

Alex squealed in response and banged his little fist on the high chair's tray. Mom rose from her seat to give him a kiss and then made her way over to Cookie on her tiny high heels. "The babies make me so happy."

"I'm glad, Mom." I glanced sideways at Mike, who was grinning broadly. He put an arm around my shoulders and drew me close. "I hope Josie won't mind if I leave the bakery a little early that day."

"Josie would never object," he said smoothly and kissed my cheek. "I won't let her."

"Huh." Nicoletta snorted. She was seated at the foot of the table next to my grandmother. "How come no one ask *me* to babysit? I take better care of babies than Muccios. And I be right at Johnny's house."

"You will be gone by then," Grandma Rosa said practically.

Thank God. Gianna's lips mouthed the words silently. It didn't appear that anyone else had noticed besides me and my grandmother, who was smiling at her.

My father's phone buzzed. He glanced down at the screen and stood quickly. "Whoops. Gotta take this one. It's important."

"You always told us no cell phones at the table," Gianna reminded him.

Dad gave her a sly wink. "I think you'll forgive me when you hear about this." He hurried into the kitchen with the phone, and the back door slammed. A second later my father could be heard shouting, "Yahoo!"

"Yahoo? He check his email?" Nicoletta wanted to know.

Gianna groaned and poured herself some more wine.

"Please don't tell me that he's landed a publishing deal or made some bestseller list. I'm not sure that I can stand the embarrassment."

"You should be used to it by now," Mike remarked as he dug into his potatoes.

"What's it all about?" I asked my mother.

Her delicate mouth formed a pout. "I have no idea. Can you believe that your father hasn't told me anything? He's been acting very strange since yesterday."

"That because he *is* very strange," Nicoletta declared. "The man always been *pazza*." She shook her finger at me. "He probably order another coffin. Just don't wind up in this one, missy."

"You always say the right thing, Gram," Johnny observed.

My father came back into the dining room and sat down, a pleased look on his face. He picked up his fork and dug into his antipasto. "Well, Nicoletta, you're not far off about the coffin."

We all stared at him, puzzled, and Mom sighed. "Really, dear. I'm happy to help you indulge your hobbies, but frankly, I think that one coffin in the house is enough. Plus, I want Alex and Cookie each to have their own rooms when they spend the night here."

"Are you really buying another coffin?" Gianna asked.

Dad filled his glass with wine and raised it in the air. "Better than that."

Gianna looked over at me and rolled her eyes. My father always had some new scheme concocted up his sleeve. We tried to humor him because in some ways he would never grow up. A big baby, Nicoletta had once said. After a time, he'd become bored and go on to something else. But the look on his face and his mannerism told me that something was different this time.

I pushed my plate away and folded my arms across my chest. "Come on, Dad. Let's hear it."

He lowered his glass, and we watched as his expression sobered. "I can't stop thinking about Eddie. He was a good friend to me, and I'd love to be able to honor his memory."

My mother patted his hand. 'That's so nice, sweetheart. What did you have in mind?"

"Well..." My father grinned slyly as he whispered something in her ear.

Mom gave a gasp and looked at him in delight. "That's wonderful!"

Oh boy. My mother and father traveled in the same circle of weirdness, so now I was really concerned. "Don't keep us in suspense, Dad. What's going on, and what does it have to do with Eddie?"

He kissed my mother's hand. "You do know that with Linda and Arthur going up the river, Terry's been left the funeral home, right?"

"Yes, Gianna was just telling me. Terry's flying in to talk to Roger about it. We're fairly certain he's going to sell."

"He already has." My father's face was glowing.

Realization set in, and I stared across the table in shock at my sister, whose face had gone as white as a bedsheet. "Dad, you don't mean—"

My father puffed out his chest in pride. "That's right, baby girl. You're looking at the new proprietor of Phibbins Mortuary, with one slight change. It's going to be called Muccio's Mortuary in the near future."

We all gaped at him for several seconds. Gianna looked like she wanted to shoot someone. Mike only shook his head in disbelief and then resumed eating with relish. Cookie gurgled at me from her bouncy seat. Johnny glanced pityingly at both Gianna and me then turned his attention back to his food. Nicoletta mumbled something under her breath in Italian that sounded like "wacko," while my mother sat there looking at my father in adoration.

It was my grandmother's reaction that surprised everyone. Grandma Rosa chuckled under her breath, and within a few seconds, she had started to roar with laughter. We all stared at her in surprise as she picked up Nicoletta's glass of wine and raised it to my father.

"Salute, Domenic," she said with a broad smile. "It is true. There is a perfect job for everyone."

RECIPES

———

Cappuccino Crinkle Cookies

⅓ cup butter
1 cup packed brown sugar
⅔ cup unsweetened cocoa powder
1 tablespoon instant coffee
1 teaspoon baking soda
1 teaspoon ground cinnamon
2 egg whites
½ cup vanilla yogurt
1½ cups all-purpose flour
¼ cup granulated sugar

Preheat oven to 350℉ . In a large bowl, beat butter with an electric mixer on medium to high speed for 30 seconds. Add brown sugar, cocoa powder, coffee, baking soda, and cinnamon. Beat until combined, scraping sides of bowl occasionally. Beat in egg whites and yogurt until combined. Beat in as much of the flour as you can with the electric mixer. Stir in any remaining flour with a wooden spoon. Place the granulated sugar in a small bowl. Roll heaping teaspoons of dough into balls and roll in sugar to coat. Place the balls 2 inches apart on parchment-lined baking sheet. Bake for 8–10 minutes or until edges are firm. Transfer the cookies to a wire rack and cool. Makes about 2½ dozen cookies.

Spiced Apple Sugar Cookies (Coffin Cookies)

1 cup unsalted butter, room temperature
½ cup brown sugar
½ cup granulated sugar
1 egg, room temperature
2 teaspoons vanilla extract
3 (0.74 oz.) packets spiced apple cider mix (e.g. Alpine brand)
3 cups all-purpose flour
½ teaspoon baking powder
½ teaspoon cinnamon
½ teaspoon salt

With an electric mixer, cream together the butter, brown sugar, and granulated sugar until fluffy. Beat in the egg, and then mix in the vanilla and spiced apple cider packets.

In a medium-sized bowl, whisk together the flour, baking powder, cinnamon, and salt. Gradually add to the sugar and butter mixture and mix until incorporated. Divide the dough in half and wrap each portion in plastic wrap. Refrigerate for 1 hour. Lightly sprinkle work surface with flour and roll out dough to about ¼-inch thickness. If dough is too hard, allow to sit at room temperature for 15 minutes. Cut out desired shapes, and place on a parchment-lined baking sheet. Refrigerate cut-out shapes while the oven preheats to 375℉ . Bake cookies for 9–11 minutes, until the edges turn golden-brown. Allow the cookies to cool on the baking sheet for 5 minutes then remove to a wire rack and cool completely before decorating.

No-Bake Peanut Butter Cookies

2 cups granulated sugar
¼ cup unsweetened cocoa powder
½ cup milk
½ cup margarine
1 teaspoon vanilla extract
1 pinch salt
½ cup chunky peanut butter
3 cups quick cooking oats

In a saucepan over medium heat, combine the sugar, cocoa, milk, and margarine. Bring to a boil, stirring occasionally. Boil for 1 minute then remove from heat and stir in vanilla, salt, peanut butter, and oats. Drop by rounded spoonfuls onto waxed paper. Allow cookies to cool for at least one hour. Store in an airtight container for up to one week. Makes about 3 dozen cookies.

Sprinkled Lemonade Cookies

1 cup butter
1 cup granulated sugar (plus ½ cup to sprinkle on cookies)
1 teaspoon baking soda
2 eggs
1 6-ounce can or ⅔ cup lemonade concentrate, any brand, thawed
3 cups all-purpose flour

Preheat oven to 400°F. Beat butter in a medium bowl with an electric mixer for 30 seconds on medium to high speed. Add the 1 cup granulated sugar and baking soda. Beat until combined, scraping sides of bowl occasionally. Beat in eggs and ½ cup of the lemonade concentrate until well combined. Beat in flour gradually with the mixer, as much as you can.

Using a wooden spoon, stir in any remaining flour. Drop dough by rounded teaspoons 2 inches apart onto parchment-lined baking sheet. Baked for 6–7 minutes or until edges are lightly browned. Cool on cookie sheet for 1 minute and then transfer cookies to wire rack. Brush them with remaining lemonade concentrate while they are hot and then sprinkle with additional granulated sugar. Makes about 48 cookies.

ABOUT THE AUTHOR

USA Today bestselling author Catherine Bruns lives in Upstate New York with a male dominated household that consists of her very patient husband, three sons, and assorted cats and dogs. She has wanted to be a writer since the age of eight when she wrote her own version of Cinderella (fortunately Disney never sued). Catherine holds a B.A. in English and is a member of Mystery Writers of America and Sisters in Crime.

To learn more about Catherine Bruns, visit her online at:
www.catherinebruns.net

Enjoyed this book? Check out the entire
Cookies & Chance Mysteries series!

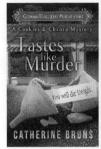 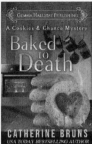 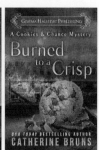

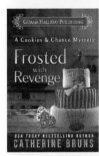 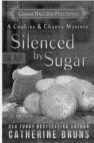 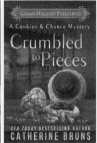

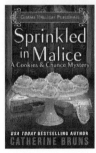  

www.GemmaHallidayPublishing.com